WOMEN AND LOVE

WOMEN AND LOVE

MIRIAM BURKE

RENARD PRESS

RENARD PRESS LTD

Kemp House
152–160 City Road
London EC1V 2NX
United Kingdom
info@renardpress.com
020 8050 2928

www.renardpress.com

'The Existentialist and the Minestrone' first published in *Bookanista* in 2020
'*Vincerò*' first published in *The Manchester Review* in 2019
'We're Not Born Here' first published in *The Honest Ulsterman* in 2019
'The Luck of Love' first published in three parts on fairlightbooks.co.uk in 2018
This collection first published by Renard Press Ltd in 2022

Text © Miriam Burke, 2022

Cover design by Will Dady

Printed in the United Kingdom by Severn

Paperback ISBN: 978-1-913724-81-8
e-book ISBN: 978-1-913724-82-5

9 8 7 6 5 4 3 2 1

CONTENTS

WOMEN AND LOVE

THE LUCK OF LOVE

M Y MIND PULLS ON any rope that ties it, so I like my job because my mind is free. My clients speak slowly, using simple words, when they talk to me. I'm an emigrant with a PhD in English Literature, but I let them think I'm uneducated and a little stupid.

The Hewitts live in North London, in a big old house with high ceilings, long windows and a garden that has been photographed for a magazine. The carved oak dining-room table came from the refectory of a French monastery and the teak four-poster bed was made in Goa. Mrs Hewitt bid for her furniture at auctions, one piece at a time, and had the damaged pieces restored. She went to artists' studios with plastic bags full of cash to haggle about the price of the abstract expressionist paintings that cover her walls. Mrs Hewitt loves the house, and everything in it, except her husband. They bought the house when it was a warren of bedsits – she showed me the photos – and she made it beautiful. The house is her life's work. Everything in her home looks like it cost much more than she paid for it, with the exception of her husband.

Mrs Hewitt worked as a solicitor, helping people buy and sell their homes, which must be a terrible job – boring legal work combined with having to deal with people at their maddest. She got out as soon as she had finished renovating and furnishing the house. Mr Hewitt is a director of a management consultancy firm.

Georgina, their daughter, is thirty years old and lives in her bedroom. She wears a lavender one-piece suit with a fur-trimmed hood, and she has the face of a child on the body of a woman. When Georgina was bullied at school, her parents employed tutors to educate her at home. It is many years since she has felt the sun on her skin. I looked at her search history when I was cleaning her room, and discovered she spends her days following female celebrities: the woman nobody knows spends her life learning about the lives of women everyone knows.

I was cleaning the kitchen cupboards last Monday morning when Mr Hewitt came into the room, dressed in a navy suit that fitted too well to be off the peg. His grey hair was as short as a newly mown lawn and his beard was carefully sculpted. His wife and daughter were sitting at the mosaic table drinking vegetable juice. I am very interested in couples, in how they survive without killing each other or themselves, so I watched and listened.

'Will you be home for supper?' asked Mrs Hewitt, without looking at him.

'I'm not sure.' He knew this would infuriate her.

Controlling her irritation, she said, 'I just want to make sure I have enough fish.'

Georgina stared at her father with the loathing her mother was concealing.

'It depends on whether I have to work late, and that depends on how often I'm interrupted. Can't you buy enough fish for three and freeze some if I can't make it?'

'It's never as good if you freeze it.'

'Put my portion in the fridge and I'll eat it when I get home if I'm late.'

'You never eat when you come home late. The meal will be thrown out.'

'Couldn't you get some steak? That'll keep.'

'Georgina doesn't eat meat any more, and I'm not going to cook two different meals.'

'I'll ring as soon as I know what's happening.' He didn't want to give her the pleasure of anticipating his absence.

'It would make life easier if you made a decision now.'

'And your life is so hard.'

Mrs Hewitt got up from the table, turned her back on him and started loading the dishwasher. Georgina glared at him and rushed out of the room.

Mr Hewitt felt guilty because he loves his sullen hermit daughter.

'I'll ring before eleven to let you know.'

'I don't care what you fucking do.'

He walked out the kitchen door, stood at the bottom of the stairs and shouted up: 'Goodbye, Georgina.'

She didn't reply.

'Enjoy your day, Georgina.'

There was no answer.

'We're lesbians,' said Margo, on the first day I met them. 'If you can't deal with that, we won't employ you.'

Every family in my country has an aunt who lives with a special friend, or a cousin who shares his life with a man he met in the army or in a bar. We don't attach words to it, but we accept them. The English seem to think they invented homosexuality.

'I'm a composer,' Margo said. She teaches piano to schoolchildren and she's been working on an opera for ten years. The opera will never be completed. She wears her hair a little wild and she tilts her head so that she resembles a bust of Beethoven.

Jo is a carpenter and she makes sets for theatre companies. She has short blond hair that stands up on her head and her fine-boned, symmetrical face is a pleasure to look at. She is about twenty years younger than Margo.

They've knocked down the internal walls of their small terraced house in South London, and put windows in the roof, and Jo has made fitted furniture for all the rooms, so the house feels much bigger than it is. They can't afford a cleaner, but they have me once a fortnight because Margo says she can't take time out from her opera to do her share of the cleaning.

I was defrosting their fridge last Tuesday while they were having a goat's cheese salad for lunch at the ash breakfast bar in the kitchen. *Der Rosenkavalier* was playing through their multi-room hi-fi system.

'Who will we invite round this weekend?' asked Jo.

'Do we have to have people every weekend, darling?' Margo stabbed a cherry tomato with her fork.

'It's fun. We work hard, and we need to play. What about Jules and Sylvia?'

Margo looked as if she had a sudden stomach cramp.

'What does that face mean?'

'Well, we do see an awful lot of them.'

'We haven't seen them for a month!'

'A month isn't very long.'

Jo put down the forkful of goat's cheese that had been on its way to her mouth.

'They're close friends. Why don't you want to see them? I thought you liked them.'

'I do like them, sweetheart. I just don't like what they do to you.'

'Do to me? I don't understand.'

'Well, you always get drunk with them and take coke and you're wiped out for the rest of the weekend.'

'It's just a bit of fun. It's good to let your hair down now and then.'

'"Now and then" seems to come around quite often... and they're so vicious about everyone. I can't imagine we're spared.'

'What do you mean?'

'Well, I wouldn't be surprised if they make fun of us when they visit their other friends. Jules is a great mimic. I sometimes think they only come to see us to get fresh material to entertain their other friends with.'

'Jules wouldn't do that to me! We've been friends since we were at school.'

'She doesn't spare anyone.'

Jo stared down at the rocket leaves on her plate, as if she was asking their advice.

She lifted her head. 'I'm not going to drop them, if that's what you want.'

'It's not what I want, darling. I'm sorry – I didn't mean to upset you.' She reached out her hand and put it on Jo's.

'I'm not upset.'

'All I'm saying is that you might find as you get older that you don't see so much of some friends because you've changed, and you may not have a lot in common any more. When people reach their late twenties they divide into two groups: the ones who continue partying like students, and they usually end up in rehab years later, and those who do something with their lives.'

'Old friends are the joists in your life – you can't discard them!'

'Some joists begin to rot with age, and they're no longer much support. Have you ever spent an evening with Jules and Sylvia when you haven't got drunk?'

'Probably not. But I don't see why that matters. I have fun with them.'

'Try it next time they come for dinner; it would be an interesting experiment.' She skewered a radish that had rolled off her fork.

'You've made your point. You don't want them to come round, so I won't invite them.'

'No, no, do invite them. I don't want to stop you seeing your friends, sweetheart. I'll go to bed after the meal and you can stay up having fun with them.'

'They'll think you don't like them if you go to bed early.'

'They'll forget about me as soon as I leave the room.'

'It wouldn't feel right staying up without you.'

'I get bored listening to the nonsense they talk when they're off their heads.'

'Jules can be very funny.'

'For half an hour, and then they both become boorish and repetitive and vicious.'

'What do I become?'

'Never vicious, sweetheart.'

'We could invite them for lunch on Sunday, and they won't stay late because they'll have work on Monday.'

'Sunday is the one full day I have to work on the opera, and...'

I left the kitchen and hurried upstairs to clean a toilet because I had heard too many of these conversations. There was no narrative tension; the outcome was always the same.

The Gilberts were eating pasta with their three children in the kitchen-diner of their newly built red-brick house in West London the evening I met them for the first time. They asked me to join them, but I said I had already eaten. Sarah Gilbert made me a coffee, using freshly ground beans, and I sat with them while they ate. She was tall and thin, with long dark hair, and would have been very beautiful if her lips had been fuller and her nose a little shorter. Her husband, Harry, was losing his hair and looked like he ate pasta too often, but it was the face of someone you'd be happy to find yourself sitting next to at a wedding.

'I'm a manager at an airline, so I'm out of the country a lot, and it isn't fair to expect Harry to do the cleaning as well as everything else when I'm away.' She looked at her husband, who smiled at her.

I liked that they felt they had to justify having a cleaner – they didn't take their privilege for granted.

'I work from home, so I'm here when the kids get back from school,' he said.

'Is there any chance you could come twice a week? It would stop things mounting up,' she said. 'These monsters do create quite a mess.'

The monsters smiled proudly at me.

'Yes, I think I could manage that; one of my clients is leaving the country in two weeks.'

'I might occasionally have to go out for an hour and leave you alone with the kids – they'll be doing their homework,' said Harry.

'That's fine. You can give me a mobile number in case there's a problem.'

'That would be great.'

'Gerry, could you try to eat your spaghetti without decorating the room with it? Twist a few strands around your fork like I showed you.'

Gerry looked about eight years old.

'You'll never keep a girlfriend if you cover her in spaghetti when you go on a date,' said Nick, who was around six years older than his brother.

'Nick is going steady,' said his mother, raising her eyebrows. 'He has dates in McDonald's.'

'Maybe Gerry will have a boyfriend,' said Florence, his sister. She was the eldest.

Gerry looked as if he was going to cry.

'It would be lovely if you had a boyfriend, Gerry,' said his mother. 'Girlfriend, boyfriend; it won't matter to us.'

'Gerry might be a girl when he grows up. We have three boys transitioning in our school,' said Nick.

Gerry looked confused. 'What's transitioning?'

'Nothing you need to know about yet, darling,' said his mother. She turned to the other two. 'For God's sake, stop teasing him.'

'Ms Chapman said it's important we have open and frank discussions about sexuality and gender. It's good for our mental health,' said Nick.

'And your father and I agree with Ms Chapman, but do we have to have these discussions when we have a guest?' She turned to me. 'They're putting on this performance for you.'

'It's fine,' I said. 'I'm enjoying it.'

She smiled at her husband to let him know that she would trust me with their children.

I looked forward to my days at the Gilberts' – I liked the noise and the energy of family life. Gerry followed me around the house, telling me about his video games; I think he missed his mother, and he wasn't allowed to interrupt his father when he was working. Nick sometimes asked me to put mousse in his hair, and to help him style it before he went on dates. Florence played me tracks by her favourite group, and showed me photos of the band members.

The children were at school one morning when Harry came into the bathroom I was cleaning and asked if I'd like a coffee. I had woken late that morning and rushed out without breakfast, so I accepted his offer. When he came back with two cups, he said, 'Have a break. Join me in the kitchen.'

I must have looked dubious: I'd had experience with neglected husbands.

'I haven't had a conversation with an adult for four days, and I'm beginning to talk like, you know, a teenager. And it ain't cool, man.'

I laughed. 'Well, it would be good to have a break.'

We sat opposite each other at the ceramic kitchen table and he passed me a packet of shortbread.

'The coffee is good,' I said.

'Life is too short for cheap wine and bad coffee. You're great with the kids – they really like you, especially Gerry. He'd go home with you if he could.'

'He's a lovely boy. They're all great.'

'Thank you. Do you have children of your own?'

I wasn't expecting the question, and tears started spilling down my face.

'I'm so sorry,' he said. 'I didn't mean to—'

'It's OK,' I said. 'I had a miscarriage – a very late one.'

'That's terrible – really awful. I know how frightened we were of miscarrying when Sarah was pregnant.'

'My husband killed himself a few months earlier; he died the night I was going to tell him I was pregnant. He was an anaesthetist, so he knew how to do it efficiently.'

'I don't know what to say. It's so… sad.'

'I didn't know there was anything wrong. I thought we were happy.' I looked out of the kitchen window at newly planted trees and shrubs.

'Was he depressed?'

'He didn't seem to be. We both loved our jobs; he was working at the best hospital in the country and I was lecturing at the university. We had a busy social life.

Nobody could believe it. I kept looking for answers, secrets he kept from me, but there weren't any. Maybe for some people this life isn't enough.'

'It's no reason to kill yourself!'

'He must have thought it was.'

'I shouldn't have brought it up… it was just my clumsy attempt at small talk. I am sorry.'

'You didn't bring it up – it's always there. He killed our child, too – that's what I can't forgive.'

'Do you think he would have lived if he'd known you were pregnant?'

'Probably. But staying alive for the sake of other people isn't much of a life.'

'No.'

'I look at other couples and I wonder how they do it – how they succeed where we failed.'

'There's a lot of luck involved. If you're very lucky, you meet someone and everything about them feels right. You don't have to work at it. Just seeing them walk across a room is a pleasure. And you'll do anything to keep them. As long as they're in your life, living is… joyful. And you don't worry about the meaning of life, or that you and everyone you love is going to die.'

'We didn't have that. We were good together, or I thought we were, but we didn't have what you have.'

'I don't think many people do. I've never met anyone else I could love the way I love Sarah. I couldn't imagine having another relationship if we split up. I remember reading a poem once that said if you think you've loved more than once, you've never loved. And I think it's true – or it's true for me.'

19

'It takes courage to love like that.'

'It takes courage to live without it.'

'I suppose it does. I thought of killing myself after I lost the baby. I thought about it a lot.'

We talked for a long time before I went back to cleaning the bathroom. I felt closer to Harry Gilbert that afternoon than I'd ever felt to another human being.

I couldn't sleep that night; our conversation was like a trapped bird flying around inside my head. The next morning I texted to say I wouldn't be coming back. I lied about having to return to my country to nurse a sick relative. I couldn't bear to see my story mirrored in his eyes, and to see what we never had. I knew he'd understand.

THINGS THAT MATTER

I LIE IN THE DARKNESS, listening to the sobbing of my cellmate. She is missing her children. A woman at the other end of the corridor is screaming; her attacker is always with her. My mind is going over and over what happened, searching for a different ending.

My limbs are accustomed to sprawling across a queen-size bed. My limbs are accustomed to being entwined with other limbs. Eight years of a narrow, stained mattress, eight years of listening to sobbing and screams. I close my eyes and see ringed plovers dancing at the water's edge and I hear the lament of the curlew.

My mother used to read to me every night – stories where women crossed wild seas to discover new lands, climbed mountains to claim them for their queen, fought wars to win justice for the oppressed and travelled to planets where they met friendly and charming aliens who had a lot to teach humans about how to live. She made up half of them. My father turned people's dreams into concrete and glass.

I inherited my father's passion; I love the simple lines of beams and struts, and the beauty of mathematical equations that keep buildings standing for centuries and stop roofs blowing off in a storm.

I was in the library looking at the syllabus for my first-year engineering course when Alice sat down opposite me and said, 'I'm looking for a fourth to play tennis tomorrow, and you look like you've got a good forehand.'

Something in her fine-boned face made me feel I wanted to protect her.

'My backhand is better, and I'm left handed.'

'Great. You're playing with me, because my backhand is crap.'

'It's freshers' week – shouldn't we be getting drunk and taking drugs?' I asked.

'Drugs are for people who have no imagination.' She took out her phone. 'Give me your number and I'll text you the address for the courts.'

It was one of those hot October days when the sun feels like a much-loved friend who has come back to say a final goodbye. The municipal courts in west London had grass growing through cracks in the tarmac and the net was rotting. Two boys kicked a football on the court next to us. Alice made up for her weak backhand with a serve that sent our opponents running for cover. We showed no mercy.

We drank cold lager in a pub garden with stone walls covered in blood-red leaves. We were high on the forgotten pleasure of sun on our skin and the triumph of winning.

'Why did you think I had a good forehand when you saw me in the library?'

'I didn't. I thought you looked like one of Caravaggio's beautiful boys, and I wanted to know you.' She put her hand on mine. 'I hope you don't mind me saying you look like a beautiful boy.'

'I've never felt the need to be a girl or a boy – I am me.'

'Will you marry me?'

'Your backhand isn't good enough.'

'I'll work on it.'

We made love a few weeks later, and it was like the continuation of a conversation we'd been having since we met. She moved into the house I was sharing a month later. Loving her was easy – too easy. University is where you should make your mistakes, when the stakes aren't high.

When we finished university I got a job in a big engineering company. I worked on extensions to private houses – lofts and side extensions. The houses were Victorian and there was never much room for the extensions. It was going to be years before I would be given anything interesting.

Alice got a job working for a children's charity. We bought a flat on a street with goldfinches singing in the lime trees and cars with baby seats; our parents gave us the money for the deposit. We often spent weekends on the coast in Dorset in a holiday home owned by Alice's parents. We'd walk for hours by the sea, watching and listening to the sea birds.

We were at a party one Saturday night and I was standing on my own when a woman with spiky blond hair, a black leather bomber jacket and a short tartan skirt came up to me.

'You're bored,' she said.

I looked at the room full of women dancing and chatting. 'It's a good party.'

'I didn't mean tonight.' Her accent was a mixture of Jamaican and East End, but I had a feeling it wasn't her real accent.

'You don't know anything about me.'

Her eyes were the colour of mussel shells and she had a tattoo that looked like a Jackson Pollock painting on her neck.

'I know you're not one of them.' She nodded towards the other women in the room. 'They're talking about property prices – you can tell by the greed in their eyes. And babies – the new lesbian accessory.'

'Why are you here if you despise us so much?'

'The door was open, so I came in. I never pass an open door.'

'What do you talk about at parties?'

'Things that matter. Give me your number and I'll send you an invitation to an exhibition of my paintings. You might want to buy one as a present for your girlfriend.'

I gave her my number. I had once dreamed of being a painter.

'I'm Lyssa. Go home and watch a good film. Anything is better than this shit.' She turned and left the room.

Two weeks later, I had a text saying: 'Exhibition tomorrow evening.' She gave the address. I lied to Alice about having a meeting with a client. I was hoping to get her a painting as a surprise birthday present – that's what I told myself.

Lyssa had a long room on the top floor of a warehouse in Dalston. Explosions of dark colours covered the walls.

One painting looked like a volcano, another a bomb site and a third was a raging sea.

'They're great,' I said. 'Very powerful. The technique is brilliant.'

'I hate the way women make small art, working with textiles and all that shit. They're frightened of taking up space.' Her black combat trousers and blue shirt were covered in paint.

I looked around the room and asked: 'When are the other people coming?'

'It's a private viewing – no one else is invited.'

A charge coursed through my body.

I followed her to the living space at the far end of the room. There was a mattress on the floor, a sink and a camping stove with a double burner. We sat on old wooden garden chairs painted the colours of the rainbow.

'How did you learn to paint so well?'

'By painting badly for a long time. And by making it the only thing in my life that matters.'

She took a small packet from her trousers and laid out two lines of coke on a yellow plate.

'Do you have a Jane Austen?' she asked.

'A first edition?' I asked, confused.

'A tenner,' she said, and mimed snorting with a note.

I laughed and took one from my jeans.

After we'd had two lines each, she took my hand and pulled me on to the bed. The blue bed linen was clean and made of very fine cotton. She lay on top of me, unbuttoned my blouse and bit hard into the flesh on my shoulder. I let out a little yelp and she laughed. She moved her hands slowly over my body as if she was stretching

25

and flattening a canvas. She stopped every few minutes and had a little bite or pressed hard on my skin.

'I'll do anything you want me to,' she whispered in my ear. 'I'll make your filthiest dreams come true.'

When her hands had finished their journey around my body, she suddenly pushed deep inside me, again and again. I felt the rope that moored me give way.

Alice was already asleep when I got home. I'd texted to say I was having something to eat with the client. I undressed in the bathroom and saw bite marks all over my body and the beginnings of bruising. I'd have to be very careful.

She woke when I got in beside her. 'How was it, sweetie?'

'Boring.'

'Poor you.'

She put her arms around me and fell back to sleep.

Betraying Alice was as easy as loving her. When friends had told me about their secret affairs, I'd never been able to understand how their partners hadn't known.

'Living with someone makes you an expert on how to deceive them,' said one friend.

I heard nothing from Lyssa for weeks. I saw her everywhere, heard her voice and smelled her paint. My disappointment was shading into relief when I saw her sitting on a motorbike outside my office one evening.

'Hop on,' she said.

'How did you know…?'

'We are all prey on the savannah of the internet.'

'Nice bike.'

'It's not mine.'

She drove fast down bicycle lanes, past the rush hour traffic, terrifying cyclists. She parked the motorbike on a footpath when we reached the Thames. I followed her down stone steps set into the river wall until we reached the stony sand. The sun was low in the grey metal December sky. We stood under a bridge, looking at the churning water and listening to the siren of an ambulance scream above us. A cormorant with outstretched wings stood on a high wooden post, watching us.

'I love it here,' she said.

She took my face in her hands and kissed me, her tongue slowly exploring my mouth. She opened my coat and moved her hand tenderly around my body while I watched the treacherous water rise.

I didn't see her again for a month, but she was with me always – inside me. I'd forgotten to turn off my mobile one night and I got a text at about 3 a.m. with the message: 'Private viewing tomorrow evening.'

'Who was that, darling? There's nothing wrong, I hope?' said Alice. She kissed the back of my neck as I was turning the phone off.

'Just a stupid ad.'

She was wearing a short, tight black silk dress with stilettos, and she was heavily made up. Her pupils were dilated and she was moving fast around the room.

'I sold a painting today, for a shit load of money.'

'Congratulations.'

'Have you ever been fucked up the ass?'

I didn't answer.

She laughed. 'You haven't – you're a virgin! Oh, I'm going to have fun tonight.'

I got used to hiding the bites and bruises. I'd always take a shower when Alice was finished in the bathroom, and I wore a T-shirt in bed.

'You seem different – happier,' said Alice, after we'd eaten one evening. 'Is work getting more interesting?'

'Yes, it is.' I didn't even have to look away any more when I lied.

'I'm glad, darling.'

I lied to the office about a site visit so that I could meet Lyssa one afternoon. When I arrived home after seeing her I had a shower, knowing Alice would be at her book club. I was stepping out of the shower when I saw the bathroom door open.

'Hi! I decided to skip book club – I hadn't finished the book.' She came closer to me, looking at me closely. 'What's happened to you? Those marks…' And then she let out a long, low animal sound that will always haunt me.

We stayed awake all night, crying and talking. When she asked how long it had been going on, I said, 'A few months.'

She pulled away from me as if I'd hit her, and she jumped out of bed.

'You've been lying to me for months!' she shouted. 'How could you do that to us?'

'I'm so sorry. I won't see her again, I promise. I love you.'

'God, I'm such an idiot. I thought you were happy because your work was more interesting. You two must have had a good laugh at how easy it was to fool me!'

'I never talked to her about you,' I said.

28

'Why didn't you tell me about it? We could have found a way through it together.'

'I didn't want to hurt you,' I said quietly.

'You didn't want to hurt me?' she screamed. 'That's funny! Very funny. Do you believe your own bullshit?'

I reached out my hand. 'Come back to bed, please.'

'She marks you like a farmer brands his animals.'

'We can handle this – we're strong enough. Please come back to bed.'

'It'll never be the same again.'

'Maybe not, but it'll still be love.'

'It's not love if there isn't trust.'

I sent a text the following morning to Lyssa saying: 'Sorry, can't go on.' There was no reply. I had to be careful not to check my phone when I was with Alice.

I was at work a week later when the receptionist phoned to say my client was in the waiting room. I wasn't expecting anyone, but I was afraid I'd forgotten to put an appointment in the diary, so I said, 'Send them up.'

She was wearing a full-length black leather coat and a silver chain around her neck. She looked around the room and said, 'Not much of an office.'

'I haven't been here long.'

She walked over to the window and, with her back to me, said, 'That was no way to finish with someone. I expected better of you.' She turned to face me. 'If you don't come with me now I'll cause a terrible scene.'

When Alice got home from work that night, she said, 'I got your favourite – fresh scallops. I think I'll cook them with ginger. Will you wash the potatoes?'

'I need to talk to you.'

'You've seen her.' She dropped the bag of scallops on the floor.

'I can't get out of it. I tried.'

'I was expecting this. We're finished.'

'I know.'

'Do you understand what you've done?' A tear ran slowly down her face.

'Yes.'

'Have any idea how lucky we were? How few people have what we had?'

'I'm so sorry.'

'Why can't you get out of it? I don't understand the hold she has over you.'

'I don't either.'

'You'll have to move out. And pay the mortgage until I can sell.'

'Of course.'

'We're losing our home, our life, our future. You've destroyed it all.'

I moved into a studio flat on a treeless street in Hackney, where I lay awake at night listening to police sirens. Alice's last words to me rang around the room. 'I loved you because you were honourable. I'll never trust anyone again.'

Sometimes I'd see Lyssa every day for a week, and other times I wouldn't see her for a month. We took coke, drank and had sex. We never ate together, went to a film or to a supermarket. She talked with contempt about domesticated love. She didn't have a car, so she'd often ask me to drive her to a friend's place to pick up something she'd left behind the night before or drop something off. I'd always wait in the car, tormenting myself with images of her making love to someone else.

We were lying in bed one Saturday morning when she said, 'I think we should go away next weekend. I was thinking Amsterdam.'

'Great. I've never been.'

'Give me your credit card and I'll book it today.'

I must have looked hesitant, because she laughed and asked, 'Don't you trust me?'

'Of course I do,' I said.

'Is it OK if I book the accommodation with your card too? I'll pay you back.'

'Go ahead.'

'It'll be cheaper if we only check in one case – bring one of yours and I'll put my stuff in it. I'll book an early flight so we have more time there.'

'We can share a cab if I spend the night before we leave here.'

'That's cool, babe.'

We were at the boarding gate when she said, 'I forgot to tell you, our seats aren't together – we were too late booking.'

'It's all right, it's a short journey.'

'That's what I thought.'

The apartment was very camp – red velvet curtains, sequinned cushions, gold taps and statuettes and paintings of naked young men everywhere. We visited a few modern art galleries in the afternoons, and a bookshop, where she bought two art books. We ate fish wrapped in pandan leaves and spicy beef at an Indonesian restaurant near the apartment, and spent the rest of the time in bed. She held my hand when we walked through the streets.

'Whatever happens, we've had this,' she said, after we'd made love on our last night there.

'What do you mean, "whatever happens"?'

'I might go and live in New York – the art scene there is great; I might decide to go straight, kill myself, give up sex. Anything could happen.'

I kept silent.

When we arrived at Heathrow, she kissed my cheek and said, 'You wait for the case, and I'll go outside and queue for a taxi.'

I watched her walk through customs, and felt desolate knowing we wouldn't be spending the night together. I had a long wait for the case – a lot of flights landed at the same time. I was agitated, knowing she hated waiting.

There were three customs officers standing behind metal tables; the only woman amongst them had a dog. As I was passing her, the dog became excited.

'Excuse me, miss, could I have a word?' she said. She was young, and she glanced over at the male officers after she stopped me, so I wondered if she was a trainee.

'Of course,' I said.

'Put your case up here. Did you pack it yourself?'

'Yes.' I thought I'd be able to move on more quickly if I didn't mention my girlfriend had packed her stuff.

'Do you mind if I open your case?'

'Not at all. Here's the key.'

The officer carefully lifted clothes with her gloved hands and felt them to see if anything was hidden. When she picked up one of Lyssa's art books, I noticed it was covered in a plastic film that I hadn't seen when I looked through it in the apartment. My body went cold.

'I'll have to take this off.' She looked directly at me to see my reaction.

'That's fine.'

She took off the film, and looked at me again before slowly opening the book.

We both stood for a few seconds staring at the two large packets of white powder that lay in the hollowed-out pages.

No one using Lyssa's name had travelled on either of my flights, and she hadn't used my credit card to book her ticket. Her studio was empty when the police checked it out, and her mobile was disconnected.

There is a certain satisfaction in serving out my sentence, because I have committed a crime: I betrayed someone who entrusted me with her life.

THE OTHERNESS OF PEOPLE

T HEY MET IN A CAFÉ with rustic wooden tables and brightly coloured woven rugs hanging from the walls.

'The coffee isn't great,' she said, 'but the piped music is baroque and the tables aren't too close to each other.'

He was the tallest man in the room and his shoulders hadn't started to turn in yet or lose their muscularity. She had inherited a prejudice against small or physically weak men from her mother and grandmother. It was primitive, and she had been careful not to pass it on to her daughter.

'I like it,' he said.

There was an intimation of kindness in his face that combined with his strength to make him very attractive to women.

'An Americano with hot milk on the side, please,' she said.

The young waitress spoke with a Spanish accent and had eyes the colour of peat.

'Same, thank you,' he said.

She had converted him to taking hot milk with his coffee thirty years earlier.

'I'm glad you contacted me,' he said.

'No one else could understand.'

'No.'

'How's Charlotte?'

'She's fine. Busy, you know.'

'Yes, everyone is so busy these days.'

She noticed how his cobalt-blue linen suit brought out the blue in his eyes. Charlotte must have chosen it, because he had never been interested in clothes. And she must have persuaded him to grow his hair longer, too. It suited him; he looked like an actor or a playwright.

'And Richard?'

'He's started a new job working for a company that specialises in entertainment law, and he loves it.'

She had always liked his voice – there was something very comforting about the timbre. It made her feel the world was safe and people were good.

'You're still working?' she asked.

'Yes. I don't take on as many clients as I used to. I heard you retired?'

'I couldn't carry on after…'

He nodded.

The waitress arrived with two bowls of coffee and one jug of milk. He turned the handle of the jug towards her.

'How are you?'

She drank some coffee. 'There are days when I feel nothing, absolutely nothing. It's as if everything inside me has been scooped out and there's only a great emptiness left.' She looked into his eyes. 'And they're the good days.'

He reached out and put his hand on hers, and they were silent for a while. The familiarity of his touch brought back too many memories; she wanted to take her hand away, but she left it lying beneath his.

'And you?' she asked.

'I think I'm all right, and then I hear a certain song and I find myself crying, great gulping crying like a child. It's always one of those awful pop songs she used to sing, like 'Shaddup You Face'.'

'Oh, God, that one was torture.'

'Where did she pick them up? You only listened to Radio 4.'

'The nanny – they used to dance to them.'

'She was such a happy child,' he said.

She leaned towards him and asked, 'But was she? I've been questioning everything. Maybe she was too happy. It might have been a front, or some kind of manic state.'

'Children don't dissemble. It's not in their interests to hide unhappiness.'

'The divorce must have had an effect.'

'We were very careful. Well, you were very careful to make sure we handled it well. And lots of couples get divorced without...'

'Do you really cry when you hear those awful songs?'

'I had to stop the receptionist listening to the radio at work.'

'You never cried when we were married.'

'I hadn't cried since Nick Walker deliberately spilled ink over my new pencil case. He works for an oil company now.'

'You don't blame yourself, do you? You don't go back over the past and wonder what you did wrong?'

'There's no point.' He looked annoyed.

'I know there isn't, but I just can't stop myself.' She put her hands around her coffee to feel its comforting heat.

'I blame myself for us breaking up. I never thought I would lose you and Clare.'

'It was the months of lies, the daily deceits that I couldn't forgive.'

'I can understand that now.' He sighed. 'It takes a life-time to learn how to live well, and by then it's too late.'

She noticed his nails were badly cut; she used to cut and file them because he didn't have the patience to do the job properly.

'She was more subdued at secondary school.'

'That did seem like a part she was playing... a part in which she was miscast,' he said.

'I kept waiting for her to get rebellious and to start hating me, but it didn't happen. Maybe the rebellion was in conforming.'

'It was easier for our generation to rebel – we had a lot to be angry about. She was much more herself at univer-sity. She seemed happy again,' he said.

'She found her tribe in the dramatic society. She loved being a student – she was able to play. I don't think either of us gave her much attention while she was away at college – I was busy with work and had met Jack, and you were splitting up from someone or other.'

'Margy – she'd left me.'

She wondered if he remembered the drunken phone call when he suggested they get back together. He hadn't known she was with someone. She'd been enraged by his arrogant assumption that she would have him back.

'Clare phoned me most days to see if I was OK,' he said.

'I didn't know that.'

He turned his head so she wouldn't see his tears.

'It doesn't matter,' she said.

'I feel worse afterwards, that's why I hate it. I don't care about the embarrassment – I'm long past that.' He wiped away a tear with the back of his hand. 'What were her university friends like?'

'They were delightful: great fun, very attractive. A group of them would come with their sleeping bags for the weekend, and I'd hear them giggling all night. There was an innocence about them.'

'I was surprised she got such a good degree; I thought she was too busy partying to do much studying.'

'She was very good at cramming – she used to take caffeine tablets.'

'I never met any of the boyfriends. What were they like?'

'Remember Cerberus?'

'How could I forget the brute? Didn't she demand the animal shelter brought out the dog they'd had the longest?'

'Yes – exactly. And he growled at her, and she instantly fell in love with him. Well, her boyfriends were like that, but they never became devoted to like Cerberus did. I don't know where she picked them up – maybe there's a special home for angry young men no one wants.'

'It's called the internet.'

She laughed.

He looked at his watch. 'Do you want to get something to eat? The restaurants will be serving dinner by now.'

She looked doubtful.

'You have to eat, and it'll save you cooking tonight. It'll be my treat.'

'There's no need to treat me. One of those television celebrity chefs – I can't remember his name – opened a new restaurant at the end of this street. It'll be expensive.'

'I don't mind expensive if the food is good.'

She nodded to the waitress to get them the bill.

Walking next to him reminded her how good it had once felt to be with him, and how confident they had been that together they would be a match for anything life could throw at them. Loving him had felt so easy. She used to feel sorry for friends who said they had to work at their relationships. She forced herself to remember the day she discovered his treachery.

When she had confronted him, he said, 'It's not important.'

'It is to me,' she had replied.

Back then she was too young to accept the messiness of love, of life.

A painting of Roman noblemen in togas feasting on animal carcasses hung from a wall of the restaurant. It was already full, and most of the tables were occupied by small groups of young women.

'These women look like the mistresses of Russian gangsters,' she said.

'They all look alike.'

'They must use the same cosmetic surgeon.'

'What's happened to our city?'

'It's the money-laundering capital of the world,' she replied.

'I always promised myself I wouldn't become one of those old people who complain the world is going to hell in a handcart – they hate to think they're leaving anything good behind. But it's tempting sometimes.'

The waiter arrived with the menus, and looked at them as if being middle-aged was a violation of their dress code.

'Would the *signore e signora* like a cocktail?'

'We'll have some wine with the meal,' she replied.

The waiter looked affronted and walked away without saying anything. He had decided their tip wouldn't merit civility.

'It's a good menu. I think I'll have the burrata with asparagus and edamame for a starter,' he said. 'If you get something different, we could share them.'

'I'd rather order what I like and not share it.'

He looked hurt, and she had to stop herself saying something to make him feel better.

'I'll have the crispy duck with five-spice dressing, toasted cashews and bean sprouts. I like to think they've had to do some cooking,' she said.

'And the main?'

'I'll have the salmon and smoked haddock fishcake.'

'And I'll have the sea bass with fennel and caper and shallot dressing.'

'I noticed a Grüner Veltliner that looks interesting…'

'Let's go for it.'

After they'd ordered, he started up again. 'What happened with that job at the magazine? She was so excited to get it, and I was never clear about why she left.'

'She realised she didn't want to spend her life editing articles about fashion and cosmetics.'

'And that's when she got involved with the cult.'

She unfolded a pink linen napkin and spread it over her knees to protect her white trousers. 'It isn't really a cult. I've done a lot of research, and I went to one of their events. It's a movement led by an Indian woman called Mata Amritanandamayi – she's known as Amma, which means mother.'

'What do they believe?'

'Amma is a Hindu spiritual leader, and she encourages qualities such as compassion, selfless service, patience and forgiveness.'

'It's hard to see what's new about any of that.'

'What's new is that she hugs people and they find that transformative.'

'Hugs them?'

'Yes, a literal hug. She has hugged more than 34 million people in over thirty years. People queue for a whole day to be held by her. I tried it; I wanted to understand what Clare got from it. Amma pulls you to her breast and says, "My daughter, my daughter," while she strokes your back. And you're given an apple and sweets to take away. It was nice to be hugged – she's a good hugger – but I didn't feel anything spiritual.' She looked down at the table. 'I suppose I felt it was a bad reflection on me that Clare chose a guru called Mother whose hugs she craved.'

'You were a good mother.'

'I wasn't much of a hugger; my parents rarely touched us.'

'Clare knew she was loved – don't ever doubt that. Is hugging all that this Amma does?'

'No, she has an international network of charitable organisations that provide food, housing, education and medical services to the poor. She has a genius for attracting funding.'

'So she's a modern-day saint?'

'Well, one of her former disciples published a book saying she's a terrible bully in private and has affairs with her monks while maintaining she's celibate. She was also accused of siphoning off money.'

'Hmm. What did Clare do at the ashram?'

'She cleaned and worked in the fields.'

'The Indians must think it's hilarious that all these rich Westerners do their cleaning and work the land for them.'

'I don't think that's how they see it.'

'It's how it is.'

The waiter arrived with their starters. He got them the wrong way around and they had to ask him for a bucket of ice to keep the wine chilled.

'Amma's not to blame for what happened.'

'She was different when she came back,' he said.

'She was disappointed; she had discovered there is no ideal society. She wanted the world to be a better place, and she couldn't bear that she wasn't able to change it. She couldn't understand why we don't give our disposable income to save children dying from hunger and treatable illnesses. She didn't have whatever it is that stops us bringing the freezing man or woman lying in a doorway into our warm homes on a winter's night. She could feel people's suffering – to her they weren't "other". She became them. It was a gift and a curse. She felt lost and alone. And I had no idea—'

He put his hand on hers. 'Neither of us knew.'

'I never told you about that morning?'

'No.'

'I suppose there was always someone else around. Do you want to hear it?'

'Yes…' There was fear in his eyes.

'I was working from home, preparing a lecture. I assumed she was up and had had breakfast. The door of my office was closed, so I wouldn't have heard her. And I was concentrating hard because I was giving the lecture that afternoon. When I went to make a coffee, I was surprised not to see her breakfast dishes. I went up to her room to see if she wanted a coffee. There was no answer when I knocked, so I opened the door, thinking she was still asleep. I knew immediately – her colour – but I shook her very hard and screamed and screamed at her to wake up. My screaming was so loud the neighbours phoned me and they called the ambulance. I went with her to the hospital. I kept begging the doctors to resuscitate her – I told them she wanted to live so they must try. But there was no point. She'd been dead for hours. I wouldn't go home. I grabbed every doctor I could find and followed them around, pleading with them. In the end, they got their psychiatrist to see me. She explained I was in shock.'

'I'm so sorry I wasn't there.' His tears had left snail trails down his face.

'She looked very peaceful; you should know that.' She had to stop herself from drying his face with her napkin.

'Thank you.'

'It was just like she went to sleep and she didn't wake up.'

'You never found a note?'

'I don't think she wanted to die, she was just desperate for some peace.'

'We can't know what's going on inside another person,' he said.

'We don't understand what's going on inside ourselves half the time.' She drank some wine.

'She inherited what was best in both of us – she was our gift to each other.'

'Her friends keep in touch with me; they miss her very much. I've had so many emails and cards.' She looked around her. 'It's strange to be talking about her in this restaurant, eating this food: she'd hate it here. She'd be railing at us for spending so much money on a meal when we could have donated it to famine relief.'

'She'd love it that we've met.'

'Yes, she would.' She took her hand from under his. 'If we don't eat, our gracious waiter will bring the main courses before we've finished the starters.'

'I need to ask you something.'

He was touching his tie, as if it was a comfort blanket.

'What is it?' She didn't want to hear the question.

'Will you see me again?'

She looked away from him. 'I don't know.'

VINCERÒ

I LOVE MY JOB. I love standing in the darkness taking in the smell of their cooking, a whiff of perfume, a trace of lemon fabric conditioner on a clean tea towel. Tony and I stand very still for a few minutes to make sure we haven't been heard. We tend to come in the garden door, which usually has a spring latch that we can open in a few seconds with a credit card. We have a bolt cutter for patio doors.

Tony moves the beam of his torch around the kitchen while we look for phones, tablets and car keys. I check the sink for watches or rings. We move very quietly from room to room; we wear the rubber-soled aqua shoes that people use to protect their feet from sea urchins. We're dressed in Puffa jackets and designer jeans so we can say we're friends of the owners if a neighbour sees us. We put on latex gloves and balaclavas before we go into the house.

Tony did a computing course so we can research our subjects – that's what we like to call them. We nick something from their letter box to get a name, and then he researches them on the internet. He can get into anyone's social-media account, and he finds out if they're going away on a summer holiday or heading to another country for Christmas. We watch a house for days before paying our visit. I did a course in art appreciation to make sure we don't miss a good painting, and I once worked for a woman who has a shop selling antique jewellery in Westbourne Grove; she told me I had a good eye. Our fences don't try to cheat us because we know what everything is worth.

Tony is my brother. Well, he's black and I'm white, so we didn't have the same parents, but he's a real brother in all the ways that count – we lived next door growing up, and his mother always fed me if our fridge was empty, and I slept on their sofa when I got locked out. His mother, Leticia, is from Barbados, and she turned our South London council estate into a Barbadian village. She looked after strays like me, and grown-ups went to her when they were in trouble. She's a big woman with a loud voice and no one messes with her – well, no one except for her husband, but he was hardly ever there.

My mother was a drunk. There should be a word for a lovely, cheerful drunk, because she wasn't like the image in your head. She'd wake me by throwing her arms around me and slur, 'I love you, darling. I love, love you, love you.' Her Longford accent never changed, because she spent all her time in Irish pubs.

'Get off me,' I'd say, pulling away from her stale whiskey breath. Whiskey and coke was her drink.

'Don't you love your poor mother?'

I'd look at the clock and say, 'I'll be late again – Sister Assumpta will kill me.'

'Feck Sister Assumpta. Stay with me today. We'll have a little party, just the two of us.' She'd start singing and I'd push her off me, pull on my school uniform and run to school.

Tony is very tall and I'm small. I can usually fit through a bathroom window, and that can save us a lot of time. Tony likes men, but he can never tell his mother because it would bring shame on her; she hopes he'll marry me. I like men too, but in small doses – I have a few days of fun and then I don't want to see them again. If I ever have a child, I'd like Tony to be the father.

'If a thing is worth doing, it's worth doing properly' – that's what Sister Assumpta used to say, and it's why we never get caught. We don't go for New Money; they could have a gun or know how to use a knife. We like the kind of people who have always felt safe in the world – people who don't have alarms because they live in a neighbourhood with a low crime rate, people who have inherited jewellery and paintings.

We taught ourselves how to use knives. We studied anatomy diagrams on the internet and we practised on stuffed bin bags. We bought filleting knives from a shop that sells kitchen equipment, and we keep them sharpened. We never work with anyone else, and we keep our business to ourselves. People can't grass on you if they don't know anything.

I was always smart, but I never did my homework, because there was always too much noise at home. My mother was forever either singing along to the radio or laughing and drinking with men she'd picked up in a pub. If she had a man staying the night, she locked me in my bedroom – until I was old enough to lock the door myself. I'd often be woken in the night by the sound of the door handle being turned.

The teachers concentrated on girls whose parents would complain if they didn't get good grades – they knew which street every family lived on, the kind of car they drove. When I asked my mother why she sent me to a convent school, she said, 'It's good preparation for life – you'll learn never to trust anyone in a position of power.' I sat at the back of the class wearing a uniform I had outgrown and a white blouse with dirty cuffs.

I decided to make friends with a quiet girl whose mother drove a Mercedes. She didn't belong to any gang, so she was easy picking. I got her to invite me back to her place after school by saying I'd like to hear a CD she'd bought. The house smelled of polished antique furniture, mixed with freesias picked from their garden and roasting meat. Her mother's eyes went cold when she saw me – you can't hide poverty – and I was never invited back.

We change our number plates before we set out on a job. We drive a silver Golf, the kind of car a wife would use to drive children to school, and we park a street away. We never do more than one job in a neighbourhood.

We tell people we buy stuff at car boot sales and markets, do any repairs and cleaning needed, and sell them on eBay for a big mark-up. We're careful not to flash too much money about. Holidays are our thing. We've been everywhere – LA, Sydney, Cape Town, Goa. We collect air miles and we always get an upgrade. We tell everyone we're going to Ibiza.

Tony's dad was Nigerian, and he would appear every few years when some woman had thrown him out, and Tony's mother would take him back because her pastor told her it was her Christian duty. His sons hated their father because he made them treat him as if he was a tribal chief. When they complained to their mother, she'd tell them they had to honour their father.

I have no idea who my father is. All I know is that when things got so bad my mother was pawning our furniture, a cheque would arrive. I figure she was blackmailing my father because she came over from Ireland to have me when she was only just sixteen, which means my father was a child abuser. He must have been a teacher, a married friend of the family, or maybe a priest – someone with a reputation to lose. I don't think she would have loved me so much if her father or brother was my father.

We store everything in a lock-up garage near our estate. We keep things a while before we pass them on to our fences. The only thing we have to shift quickly is cars: we have a contact who has them out of the country within twenty-four hours. We make serious money from luxury cars. Our fences know nothing about us, so we don't worry about them getting nicked. We take it in turns to contact them, and they don't know we're working together.

My mother's memory was shot by the time she was fifty. I took her out of the nursing home the council put her in because I didn't like how the staff talked to her. I found a private home with a bar for the residents and I top up the fees paid by the council. She started singing again when she moved there. She thinks I'm one of the nurses.

Tony moved into the flat with me when my mother was taken away. We spent two weeks scrubbing the floors and painting walls, and we ordered a truck full of furniture from a Danish design shop with the proceeds from a BMW convertible that was only a few months old. I worry sometimes that Tony will meet someone and move out, but the kind of guys he likes aren't interested in marrying a black boy from a council estate.

We never talk about what would happen if we're caught. I sometimes wake in the night and imagine what it would be like to be locked away for the best years of my life, to be trapped in a prison full of mad fuckers (I watched every episode of *Bad Girls*). My mother would have to leave the nursing home, and I wouldn't be able to see her. And I think about what would happen to Tony in a men's prison, and I know he wouldn't survive it.

We're doing a big detached red-brick house near Wandsworth Common tonight. We watched the family load their suitcases into a four-wheel drive a few days ago. The garden door is so easy it's insulting. Tony decides the downstairs toilet is the easiest way in, so he jimmies it open and gives me a leg up after we've put on our gloves and balaclavas. I slide over the toilet on to the floor and do a handstand to celebrate. I let Tony in through the sliding door that leads from the kitchen diner into the garden.

Tony turns on his torch as soon as he gets in because we know the family is away. We're not expecting phones or computers, so we're looking for jewellery, paintings and anything gold or silver. I've been researching valuable books, so I might have a look for some first editions. The steel kitchen counters are clear and the polished concrete floor is spotless. I open the fridge door and see there's no fresh food or milk.

Rugs with brightly coloured geometric shapes cover the floorboards in the dining area. We move quietly around the huge room. I stop to look at photos on the piano: children are riding horses through a wood and skiing down a mountain. There's a wedding photo, and I imagine the expression on the couple's faces when they get back from their holiday.

Tony lifts up paintings to see if there's a safe in the wall. I'm walking towards a bookshelf when I trip on a small plastic car and knock over a standard lamp; it's metal and makes a loud noise when it hits an uncovered floorboard.

'It's just as well there's no one here,' I say.

A landing light comes on before Tony has a chance to answer. He switches off his torch and we stare at each other, unable to do anything for a few seconds. I pull a knife from an inside pocket and Tony takes out his knife, too. We stand very still. I say a Hail Mary that whoever it is will go back to bed. My legs feel as if the strings operating them have been cut.

'Is there someone there?'

A man in burgundy silk pyjamas walks slowly down the stairs; he's the man in the wedding photo. He flicks on the light switch at the bottom. When he sees us in our balaclavas and holding knives, he says, 'Oh, God, I have children. You can take anything you like. Please don't kill me.'

His fear calms me. We've rehearsed what to do, but I'm struggling to remember the steps. I see Tony pull a set of handcuffs from his pocket and lock the man's hands behind his back, and I take a roll of tape from my pocket and try to stop my hands shaking while I tape his mouth. We work in silence. Tony ties an imaginary knot with his hands to let me know we need something to put around the man's legs. I move about the room and find a wool scarf hanging at the end of the banister. We lead the man to the sofa and make him lie down so that Tony can tie his feet.

Tony nods towards the stairs to let me know he's going up to see what he can find. I'm torn between wanting to get away as quickly as we can and not wanting to leave with nothing. I don't stop him. He's disappeared up the stairs before it occurs to me there might be someone else up there – someone who could have phoned the police.

'Fuck.' I say it quietly.

I stand over the man with the knife in my hands and I look at his chest, remembering the anatomical diagrams. He sees where my eyes are focused. He tries to speak through the tape. I bring the knife closer and he goes quiet. With one jab, I can wipe out everything he is – all his memories, his feelings and his thoughts. I can take away his past, his present and his future. I'm enjoying the fear in his eyes. I touch the blade of the knife with a finger and I smile. He thinks he's done no harm, he thinks he's led a good life, but he's guilty, guilty as hell.

Tony comes back down ten minutes later and his eyes tell me he's happy. His backpack is bulging. If there was someone else up there he has dealt with them. He moves quickly to the back door and I follow him. I open the fridge on my way out and take a bottle of champagne I spotted earlier.

We can't wait to start celebrating, but Tony drives home carefully, because we know this is when we could blow it all by getting caught for speeding or drink driving. I hear a siren and see a police car coming towards us. I slide down my seat so I can't be seen.

'Don't change your speed or look in their direction.'

The sound of the siren grows quieter.

I sit up and turn on the car's stereo. I skip until I find Tony's favourite, 'Nessun Dorma'. We sing along at the top of our voices: '*Vincerò, vincerò.*'

YOU NEVER REALLY KNOW

W E WERE WALKING in the park one Sunday afternoon when he threw the grenade into our lives. Our fifteen-year-old daughter was visiting a friend and our thirteen-year-old son was at home playing *Fortnite*. The wet branches of the plane trees shimmered in the winter sun and herons stood hunched by the frozen lake as if they were meditating on the transience of living things. We had made love that morning, and our hands touched as we walked. He stopped when we reached the Buddhist shrine on the path by the river, and that's when he said, 'There's something I need to tell you.'

I felt no alarm – I trusted my husband.

'I... I think I'm a woman. No, I... I know I'm a woman.'

I laughed. 'Very funny, but that isn't something you should joke about.'

'I'm not joking. I am a woman.'

I stared at my six-foot-two husband, at his beard, the swimmer's shoulders under his long winter coat, his size-eleven feet.

'It's not possible – you'd have known before now.'

'I've always known.'

I felt as if I'd fallen through the ice on a frozen lake. 'I don't understand.'

'I've always known my body was wrong. I knew as a child I should be playing with the girls. What I see in the mirror isn't who I am inside. I hate what I see; I can't live with it any more.'

I saw in his eyes that this was his truth and I couldn't touch it.

I grabbed his arm.

'What about us – me and the children?'

'I love you. I love the children. I'm happy with you, but I've never been happy with myself. I want us to stay together.'

'Why now? Why are you telling me now?'

He looked away. 'I've decided to transition.'

I pulled back from him.

'You can't…' I started to sob. 'You can't do this to us!'

He reached out to hold me, but I pushed him away.

'I'm sorry,' he said. 'I'm sorry.'

'You'll destroy everything.'

'Other families deal with it.'

'But the children… you'll ruin their childhood!'

'I can't carry on. I've lived a lie for forty years, and I need to be who I really am.'

'You shouldn't have married me.'

'I thought I could do it.'

'What else haven't you told me?'

'Nothing. We have a good marriage.'

'It was based on a lie. A huge fucking lie.'

'I didn't know what to do!'

The path was becoming crowded with families who had come out to walk their dogs and children after Sunday lunch.

'We've worked hard to build a decent life, and you're going to blow it to pieces because of... because of some fantasy you have about being a woman.'

'It's not a fantasy – I've been diagnosed with Gender Dysphoria.'

'By whom?'

'A specialist NHS clinic. I've started treatment.'

'More deceit and lies!' I was shouting now.

'I wanted to be sure before I told you.'

'It's cruel! It's too cruel.'

'I'll still be the same person.'

'You're a bastard – a narcissistic bastard.' I started sobbing again.

A young woman came up and asked if I was all right; she glared at Bill.

'I'm OK,' I said. 'Thanks.'

'Let's go home,' said Bill. 'We'll talk tonight.'

I nodded. I didn't want to hear any more.

We walked back in silence. I found myself staring at the pavement slabs as if they were going to rise up and hit me. I caught a glimpse of Bill's face as we crossed a road; he looked relieved.

I ran up to my son Louis' bedroom when we got home, and I bent down and hugged him for a long time. He laughed and said, 'What terrible thing have I done to deserve that?'

'How are you doing?'

'I've earned lots of points.'

'Explain the rules to me again.'

'Old people's brains don't have many gigabytes, do they?'

'We were an early design.'

'I will have completed this game in a few minutes – I'll explain it then.'

I watched his sweet face while he played, knowing his childhood was about to end. I'd wanted them to go out into the world with the confidence that only love can give and the optimism of children who haven't suffered.

When Florence got back, I was in the kitchen, chopping onions for a tomato sauce. Bill was in the study, working on his laptop. He had said he needed to finish a contract before a meeting in the morning, but I didn't believe him.

'How was your sleepover, darling?'

'Children have sleepovers.' Her subtle beauty was always half hidden behind her long black hair.

'Excuse me. How was your overnight stay at your acquaintance Miss Blackburn's?'

'Very enjoyable, thank you.'

'What did you do?'

'Played music, hung out, you know.' She took a yogurt from the fridge. 'Her parents are a bit weird.'

'In what way?'

'They seem cross with each other all the time, but Phoebe acts as if it's normal.'

I was about to say 'You must invite her to stay here', but I stopped. I felt such a surge of anger the knife in my hand started shaking.

Bill and I stayed downstairs in the living room after the children had gone to bed. He put on a Liszt sonata.

'It'll stop them hearing us.'

'Off,' I said.

'OK, OK.'

'It's only a few years until they go to university – why can't you wait till then?'

'I have to do it now. I couldn't... survive that long.'

I looked at the table made of old pine that we'd bought together at an auction, the seascape we'd taken out a loan to buy and the rugs we'd brought back from Marrakesh. 'We shouldn't haven't have had children.'

'I tried so hard, for so long, to be what you wanted. I just can't do it any more.'

'What changed?'

'I found myself thinking about it all the time and...'

'And what?'

'I started wearing women's clothes, and it feels so... right. I knew then I had to do something.'

'You were wearing women's clothes in this house?'

'When everyone was out.'

I felt sick.

'Have you given any thought to the children? To what this is going to do to them?'

'Children are adaptable.'

'How would you have felt if your father dropped you off at the school gate looking like a drag queen? Do you think your schoolmates would have been sensitive and empathic? Stop kidding yourself. You couldn't have found a better way to destroy their childhood and fuck them up. They'll be told their father is a freak and they'll be bullied. The one thing children want above anything is to be like everyone else.'

He didn't say anything for a while. I stared into the ashes left by the previous night's log fire and I felt a terrible longing for a cigarette, even though I had given them up before getting pregnant with Florence.

'We have to tell them. I need to live as a woman for a year before they'll consider me for surgery.'

'Me, me, me… What about us?'

'I can move out if that's what you prefer. It's not what I want.'

'So they'll have to deal with divorce as well as seeing their father turn into a woman.' I didn't want him to leave. 'I need a week to deal with it myself before I can handle them knowing.'

'OK.' His mouth hardened in the way it always did when he was angry.

'What did you expect? Did you think I'd be pleased for you?'

'I didn't think you'd take it this badly.'

'I'm going to bed.'

As I was walking to the door, I turned and said, 'If you really want to feel like a woman, do all the cooking, the shopping and the housework. And have your body ravaged by childbirth.'

I lay awake all night, quietly sobbing. He tried to put his arms around me, but I couldn't feel the closeness of the body he was going to mutilate, the body I had loved.

He shaved his beard the following morning, and I saw again the face of the boy I had fallen in love with.

It was my second year at university, and I was in the college bar one night with my friend Cheryl.

'Have a look at a quarter to,' she said.

I turned to my left and saw a table of muscular guys, all wearing the same tight, short-sleeved navy T-shirts.

'Tasty. Who are they?'

'Swimming team. They had a big win today; I think we should go over and congratulate them.'

'It's our duty.'

His eyes were the colour of seaweed, his black hair shone with health and his smile had none of the cynicism of other boys. I was thrilled when he moved so that I could sit next to him.

'Congratulations – I hear you won today,' I said.

'We weren't expecting it, so we're very happy.'

'You must train a lot.' I stared at the muscles in his arms and shoulders.

'Every morning. And we have to give this up when we're training.' He nodded at his pint of lager.

'You must love it.'

'It's nice to feel part of something, a team.' He noticed my empty glass and asked, 'Would you like a drink?'

'Thanks, same as you.'

When he came back with the drinks, he asked, 'What are you studying?'

'Russian and English.'

'Lucky you. I loved *Anna Karenina*.'

'Isn't it brilliant? But what a terrible ending – I wish Tolstoy hadn't killed her.'

'Her big mistake was marrying Karenin.'

'Marriage wasn't about love in those days. No one married for love.'

'She should have picked someone who wasn't such a prig.'

63

We talked all evening about tragic heroines in literature. He quoted long passages from *Middlemarch*. I was surprised when he told me he was studying law, and I asked why he wasn't studying literature.

'Genes. My father and grandfather were lawyers. It's a genetic mutation.'

It never occurred to me back then that he read novels about women because they allowed *him* to be a woman.

I was getting dressed the following Sunday when he said, 'We should talk to them today.'

'Friday night would be much better – they'll have all weekend to deal with it.'

He looked angry.

'I'm not your stepmother, trying to stop you going to the ball. You're supposed to be a bloody grown-up.'

'Don't patronise me.'

I was irritable with him all week. I knew it was making the children uneasy, but I couldn't control it. I tried not to be in the same room with them.

The following Friday night, after we'd eaten, we settled in the living room, waiting for the beginning of a talent show we always watched together.

'Children, your father has something he wants to tell you.'

'Can you be quick, Dad? The show starts soon,' said Florence.

Bill got up and started pacing near the door. The children were on the sofa and I was in an armchair next to them.

'What I have to tell you is going to be a bit of a shock, but I want you to know that I love you both very, very much.' He was becoming tearful.

'You're not getting divorced?' said Florence, looking incredulous.

'No, not that.' He put his arms behind his back as if he was going to dive into a pool. 'I'm going to become a woman. I am a woman inside, and I'm going to start living as a woman.'

The children looked bewildered.

'You're old, Daddy. It's young people who do this,' said Florence.

'Old people do it too, Florence. People didn't talk about it when I was young, and doctors didn't understand it very well and it wasn't easy to do it then. A lot of older people are doing it now.'

There was a silence, and then Florence asked, 'Will you still drive us to school?'

I could see the fear in her eyes.

'I'll drive you both to school from now on,' I said. I'd have to rearrange all my nine o'clock meetings.

'Will it be a secret?' asked Florence.

'It's not a secret – I'll be wearing women's clothes going to work and everywhere I go, so you can tell anyone you like.'

'Your father and I have arranged meetings with your schools this week to tell them about the change.'

'Louis, you haven't said anything. What are you thinking?' asked Bill.

'You'd look funny dressed as a lady, Daddy.'

'I'll get better at it. And I'll be taking hormones that'll help me look more feminine, and later I'll have surgery.'

I was furious when he mentioned surgery, because I'd asked him not to talk about it.

'It'll take a while for us to get used to it,' I said. 'Other families have much worse to deal with – loved ones get sick and die or are killed in an accident. We've been very lucky so far, and we'll help each other through this.'

'When will you start dressing like a woman?' asked Florence.

'On Monday.'

Florence started to cry and Louis' eyes became vacant, as if he was no longer present. I went over to the sofa and put my arms around them. Bill stared into the seascape on the wall opposite him.

'Let's watch the show,' I said. 'We never miss it.' I wanted them to know that some things wouldn't change.

He was in the bathroom at six the following Monday morning. When he emerged an hour later, he didn't look as bad as I expected. The hair on his blond wig turned in below his ears, his eyebrows were plucked and he was heavily made up. His satin purple blouse fitted him well, and he wore a simple black skirt with grey tights and black pumps. He looked at me with the vulnerability of a child.

'The clothes fit well, actually. Where did you get them?'

'A catalogue "for the larger lady". What do you think of the make-up?'

'You could tone it down a bit. Ditch the liner – it's very nineteen sixties.'

'I'm scared,' he said.

'No one is making you do this. You can change your mind.'

He was silent for a moment. 'The alternative is more dangerous.'

He was out most evenings – he had appointments with a voice coach, sessions with a counsellor and meetings of a support group. I'd catch him staring at me in a strange way sometimes, and I was sure he was studying how to be a woman. 'Don't!' I'd say. And he'd look away. The kids were moody, but I wasn't sure if it was normal teen stroppiness or if they were upset about their dad. Louis was becoming a man at a time when his father had decided to have his maleness surgically removed.

People stared at us when were out together. I think they assumed I was a lesbian with an outsize, ugly girlfriend, or maybe they realised my husband was wearing women's clothes. We were walking back to a tube station after seeing a play in Dalston one night when a group of young men started shouting at us from across the road. The street was dark and deserted and there was little traffic on the road. We walked quickly to get away from them, but they crossed to our side of the street and followed us. They were jeering and shouting. I only heard a few words – 'dyke... fuck...' – and was scared that they could be carrying knives.

'We should run, 'I said.

'They'll be much faster.'

I heard their voices getting closer.

'We can't just wait for them to catch up with us. We should phone the police.'

'Don't let them see your mobile.'

He suddenly caught my arm and pulled me into a side street.

'Now, run. There's a pub around the next corner. I know this area.'

He raced past me, but slowed when he realised he had left me behind.

'Hurry, hurry.'

I turned and saw the men standing at the end of the street, deciding whether to follow us. I ran so fast my phone and a set of keys fell out my bag. I didn't stop to pick them up.

We rushed in the door of the darkly lit pub, and the barman looked wearily at us, as if all his customers were fleeing imminent danger.

'I'll book an Uber. You get the drinks,' Bill said.

I had to stop myself from saying, 'Now you know what it feels like to be a woman.'

Bill's parents refused to see him unless he wore men's clothes, and my father treated him as if he was playing a practical joke. My mother was dead. Our friends divided into those who had a prurient fascination with our situation and those who gradually stopped returning calls.

Bill seemed elated most of the time, and I felt as if he was having an affair but the other woman was inside him.

'Why don't you come to a support group for families?' he asked one night. 'I know this isn't easy for you.'

'What happens at the group?'

'It's a social group where patients and their partners meet for coffee at the clinic. It's a chance to meet other people who are going through the same thing.'

'I'll go once and see what it's like.' I didn't want my anger to be seen as the problem.

There were about thirty people in the brightly lit meeting room. The pale wood chairs had a blue cloth seat covering, and posters with health information hung from the walls.

The patients were mostly men who were transitioning, and I was surprised at how many of their partners were male. Bill was embraced by a very camp Brazilian wearing a wig of back-combed blond hair and a tight-fitting silver dress with purple sequins and matching stilettos. I wasn't feeling at ease, and his exaggerated femininity reeked of misogyny to me. A few other men wearing vampish clothes joined us; Bill seemed to know them well. He was speaking in his new voice – a high-pitched whisper.

I went over to a woman sitting on her own who looked as tired as I felt.

'See the fat one over there in the dress with pink roses?' she said. Her long grey hair needed cutting and her fingers were stained with nicotine.

I looked at a man who was short and round enough to pass as a middle-aged woman. I nodded.

'That's mine. He dresses like his mother. It's a waste of time trying to understand it. God, I wish I could have a fag. Which one is yours?'

'The one in the striped blouse.'

'She's a whopper.'

I laughed so loudly I had to rush to the loo in case anyone thought I was laughing at them.

'Thank you,' I said, when I got back. 'I needed that.'

'Me and the kids laugh about it all the time. What else can you do?'

She told me stories about her childhood, growing up with a father who worked for the Kray twins. She was very entertaining.

'Come back again,' she said, as Bill took me away to meet a member of staff.

When the meeting was over, Bill said, 'Do you fancy a drink? There's a nice wine bar near here.'

'I could do with one.'

'How did you find the meeting?' he asked as we walked up the road.

'Interesting.'

'The kids could come.'

'They're confused enough.'

The wine bar had dark wooden panelling on the lower half of the walls and old farm tools hanging from the upper half. We sat at a table made from an old oak barrel and I looked at the wine list.

'It's nice here,' I said.

'I thought you'd like it.'

'There's something comforting about wood.'

A waiter walked towards us, smiling.

'Hello! I haven't seen you for a few days. How are you?'

He had a Spanish accent and his tight, lime-green shirt displayed the fruits of time spent at the gym.

'I'm good. Have you been busy? Is your colleague still off sick?'

I recognised something about Bill's face as they chatted, and it took a few seconds for me to realise what it was – it was how he used to look at me.

When I see young couples with children in the street, I think to myself, you never really know what's going on inside another human being, no matter how close you think you are.

LOOKING OUT

I STAND ON THE CEMENT FLOOR and look for my dressing gown. The last tenants took the lino and I can't afford to replace it. I don't open the curtains, because I never look out of the windows of our twentieth-floor flat. It's not natural to live so high up – living in caves is natural. But it was the only flat they offered that was near my mother when her emphysema got worse and she needed me to do her shopping. I could apply for a transfer, but the kids like it here. It's the only home they remember.

I've always been fat, except for a few thin years when I was looking for a boyfriend, and I have a wart on my face that seems to get bigger with age. I don't look in the mirror.

I put on a saucepan of porridge and make a pot of tea. I drink the tea at the metal garden table I found outside a house; I enjoy having this time to myself before I wake the kids. Robbie is in his first year at secondary school and Skye will be seven next week. Robbie is going to a Catholic school a few miles away, because I know what happens to boys from this estate who go to the local school – I've heard the screams of mothers when they're told

71

their sons have been shot or stabbed. Priests have done terrible things to boys in the past, but the school gets great results, and I tell myself they wouldn't get away with it now. It's a risk I have to take to give him a chance.

I haven't decided yet on a secondary school for Skye. I'd prefer to send her to a girls' school, because she's very pretty and she'll get too much attention in a mixed school.

I have a great head for figures. My father always took me to the pub to keep the score for his darts games because I was faster than any of the grown-ups, and I never got it wrong. And my mother used to get me to work out the cost of her shopping before we got to the checkout. I was always first to finish maths exercises in class, but I was very quiet so no one noticed. I left school at sixteen because that's what everyone did, except the emigrant kids. They did A levels, went to university and we never saw them again. My parents thought people like us weren't wanted in universities. Whoever met a doctor, a teacher or a lawyer who talked like us? I suppose they knew they'd lose me if I went into that other world. I've been thinking a lot about these things since I had my kids.

We had a good life when my father was working. He earned decent money working on building sites, and my mother did some cleaning. One day a crane he was operating toppled over and he was trapped underneath. He left the hospital in a wheelchair and my mother had to give up her work to look after him. The building company had no insurance. We lived in a council flat and the neighbours were great: they'd often buy food for us when they were doing their shopping and give it to my mother when my father wasn't looking – he was very proud. He hated being disabled. He died two years after the accident.

My neighbours are Stans: Mr and Mrs Afghanistan are on one side, and Mr and Mrs Pakistan are on the other. I'm lucky, because the Stans don't sell drugs, have drunken fights or play music all night with their windows open. We say hello when we meet in the hallway, but we'll never be friends because they think a woman with two children and no husband is a slag, and I don't want friends who think I'm a slag.

Debbie is my friend, and she's another reason to stay here. She was brought up in a big house in the country, but she became a junkie and ended up in a loony bin. She has two kids that were taken from her for a while. Her family are still rich but they won't have anything to do with her. She looks different to everyone else around here; she's very tall for a woman, her hair is naturally blond, her teeth are straight and she moves like she's dancing. She's got a lovely voice, too – there's music in it, and she doesn't swallow half her words like we do. I could listen to her all day, and sometimes I do. She talks about books and classical music, and she introduced me to radio stations where the presenters don't assume you're an idiot. Sometimes we take the kids to museums and galleries, and she knows all about the painters. We'll die together if there's a fire – she'll come up to me with her boys, we'll put on music we love, and we'll jump with the kids. We're working on a playlist. We don't fancy being cremated while we're alive.

I was asleep one night three years ago when I heard banging on my front door. I assumed it was someone looking for the drug dealer on the floor below, so I ignored it, but then I heard Debbie's voice.

'Let me in, quick!' she shouted. She was dressed and she had her two small boys with her.

'What's wrong?' I asked. I searched her face for bruises.

'They're coming to take the boys – they're going to kill them,' she said. 'They've been watching us and they follow us everywhere. They have cameras in the flat – I can't go back. You've got to hide us.'

I put the boys to sleep in my bed and I stayed up all night listening to her and drinking tea. We went to her GP the next morning and he arranged for a psychiatrist to visit my flat that afternoon; she put Debbie on drugs that made her very sleepy but stopped her talking about the men who were going to kill her boys. She and the boys stayed with us for a few weeks. She still takes the drugs, but a lower dose, so she doesn't get so sleepy.

I finish my tea and go to the kids' room to wake them. I'll have to put up some kind of partition to divide the room now they're getting older.

'What's for breakfast?' Robbie asks as soon as I wake him.

'Porridge.'

They both groan.

'Not again!' he says.

'I've put honey in it to make it sweet.'

'It's still porridge.'

'You'll thank me when you're big and strong and all the girls are after you.'

'He'll never get a girlfriend – his socks smell!' said Skye.

'Throw them in the washing basket. There are clean ones in the cupboard.' I pull off their duvets and shout,

'Up, up, you'll be late for school! If you get up now we'll have Coco Pops at the weekend.' I've seen them at the food bank.

A group of young guys jeer at us as we walk through the estate. They make fun of Robbie for walking with his mother. I shout back. It's important to let them know you're not intimidated.

We drop Skye off at her school, which is near the estate. She's very early, but the schoolyard is already full of the kids of working mothers. I go with Robbie on the bus to his school. He hates me doing it, but I'm making sure he doesn't mix with trouble. Good boys become gang members all the time in defence of their sisters. He makes me sit at the far end of the bus so no one knows I'm his mother. Grown-ups don't take the bus at this time because they can't stand the noise of the kids. A group of girls bursting out of their marine-blue school uniforms shout insults in Nigerian accents at a good-looking white boy in the same uniform, who struts up and down the bus singing rap into a rolled-up school book. I look out of the window at women driving their kids to private schools in those huge four-by-fours, and I picture their carpeted houses where everyone has their own room.

I'm drinking tea and reading a free newspaper when Debbie drops by. She won't drink instant coffee, so I pour her some tea. She's wearing a pale-blue cashmere jumper she got in a Chelsea charity shop. The staff put things aside for her. She's put on a lot of weight since she started taking the medication, but she's still a lovely-looking woman.

'Marcus came by.'

'How was it?'

'He left me some money.'

'It must have been good.'

She laughs. 'I don't feel comfortable with him leaving money after we've had sex.'

'He's leaving it for the kids, presumably – they're both his, aren't they?'

'He thinks they are.'

'I always thought—'

'I tell the kids he's their father because I don't want them obsessing about who it is – and he might be… but then again, he might not be. I was using then, and my memories are… blurry.'

'How much did he leave?'

'Two hundred.'

'You could pay off the moneylender.'

I try to help her budget, but it doesn't seem to make any difference. She says going to France when she was young and seeing them using different bits of paper to buy things destroyed her belief that money is real.

'I know.'

'Ask Marcus to pay money into your post-office account.'

'He won't have anything to do with accounts. And he hates being told what to do.'

'You could do a lot better than Marcus, Debbie.'

'I like that he's not there in the morning. And I don't have to wash his underwear. It suits me.'

I sigh. 'It must be nice to feel someone's arms around you.'

'It is.' She touches her scarred wrist – something she always does when she's nervous – and goes on, 'Something else happened since I saw you.'

76

We saw each other the day before.

'What?'

'A cousin got in touch to tell me my father is dying.'

'Oh, Debbie, I'm so sorry. Will you go and see him?'

She shakes her head. 'He won't want to see me.'

'Are you sure?'

'I did some terrible things. He'll never forgive me.'

'You can't have been that bad.'

'I stole his debit card, and I knew his pin, so I took huge sums of money and never paid him back.'

'Well, he wasn't going to starve, was he?'

'I did worse than that… much worse.'

'What?'

'I told his wife he was having an affair, and it ended his marriage.'

'Wasn't it his fault for having the affair?'

'He wasn't having an affair. He was madly in love with his wife – she was the love of his life. But I wanted to wreck their marriage. Neither of them married again. I ruined both their lives.'

I must have looked shocked.

'Bad, isn't? I hated him because he dumped my mother and won custody of us because he could afford better lawyers. But children bored him, so he packed us off to boarding school when we were very little. My mother drank herself to death alone in a small flat while he had loads of affairs and lived in luxury in his Georgian country house.'

'It's like a soap.'

'A soap written by a sadist. The only thing he'd do if he saw me at his bedside is curse me, and I wouldn't blame him.'

'You were an addict at the time.'

'The As are always banging on about how you have to accept responsibility for what you did when you were using.'

'They're tough, the As.'

'The enemy is powerful.'

'I suppose you're right. I don't really get addiction. I tried dope once; it made my knees go weak and I felt really dizzy.'

'You need the genes for it.' She sighs. 'A drug honeymoon is like no other. The world is the most enchanted, thrilling place – other people are fascinating and very sexy, and you are completely adorable and capable of anything. You have a few weeks of that, and then spend the rest of your life trying to recapture it.'

'I could do with a bit of that.'

'Drug campaigners never tell people about that part, so kids don't believe anything else they say. Kids need to be told the whole truth: that drugs are both the best and the worst thing in this world.'

'Will you go to the funeral?'

'No, I couldn't bear to meet all the mistresses again – and my polo-playing cousins.'

'You're looking healthy and lovely.'

'I look like I've been inflated with a bicycle pump.'

'Do you think he'll leave you any money?'

'He'd assume I'd use it on drugs; he doesn't know I'm clean.'

After a few hours chatting, we go to a discount store to buy food. I take out half of what she puts in her trolley; she shops as if she's preparing for a siege. We go back to her flat and she makes us sandwiches with some fancy Italian ham she managed to hide from me, and we have coffee made from real beans. I set off from there to pick up the kids.

Robbie is always waiting at the school gates when Skye and I walk from the bus stop to pick him up. We turn around when we see him and walk back to the bus stop, and he follows at a distance. But there's no sign of him today. We walk towards the gates and wait on the other side of the road, watching until the last kid comes out. A cold feeling comes over me. I take Skye's hand. 'He might be inside, talking to a teacher,' I say, as much to myself as to her.

I check my mobile in case the school has tried to contact me, but there's no message. Robbie doesn't have a mobile – I promised he could have one if he did well in his end-of-year exams.

The huge glass doors of the newly built school are locked, and there's no sign of anyone inside the building. I press hard on the buzzer, but I know there's no one to hear it. I see Robbie lying on an operating theatre with blood pouring from stab wounds. 'Stay calm,' I say to myself, 'don't scare Skye.'

'They must have let his class out early – he'll be waiting at home for us. He has his keys.'

'He doesn't always take them with him.'

My body feels as if I'm weighed down with cement blocks. I grab Skye's hand again to feel its warmth.

'He'll go to Auntie Debbie's if he can't get in.' My voice is a few pitches higher than usual.

We hurry back to the bus stop.

I can't bear how slowly the bus crawls through the traffic – we should have got a cab. I think of what could happen to Robbie if he's wandering around the estate without his keys. I feel Skye trembling; I look at her face and realise she's crying.

'What's wrong?'

'I'm scared.'

I put my arm around her and say: 'Robbie will be fine – he's very smart. He can look after himself.'

But he's never had to look after himself, because I've protected him so much. Maybe I've done it all wrong.

We run from the lift to our front door. My hands shake as I put the key in the lock. We rush into every room, but there's no sign he's been back. I find his keys next to his bed. I ring Debbie but there's no reply. She'd have phoned me if he was with her.

'He'll have gone to a school friend's house to play video games. I'll kill him for not getting someone to phone me!'

My head is full of newspaper stories about boys being abducted. They're often sons of single mothers. I'd ring the priests, but I only have the number for the school. If I phone the police, they'll say thirteen-year-old boys are often late home from school. But if he's been taken by a murderer there might still be time to save him. I pick up my phone.

The policeman doesn't seem to think it's too soon to call, and he asks for my details. His voice changes when I give him the address. He's thinking, 'What can you expect if you're bringing your kid up in that jungle?' He tells me to call back in a few hours if Robbie hasn't turned up, but I know we've been classified as low priority.

'I'll ask the Stans if they've seen him. Will you stay here in case he comes back when I'm out?'

'Yes, Mum.'

'You could start on your homework so you won't have to do it later.'

'I'm too scared, Mum.' She starts to cry. 'I had a fight with him this morning.'

'Sweetheart, brothers and sisters fight all the time. It has nothing to do with him not being here.'

I hold her and stroke her head.

'I'll put the telly on to keep you company. I'll only be a few minutes.'

Mrs Afghanistan answers the door.

'My son…'

She nods and leads me into their front room. There are brightly coloured rugs on the floor and a throw with a pattern of flamingos covering the sofa. Robbie is sitting at a table by the window, playing chess with Mr Afghanistan. Tears speed down my face as if a starting flag has been lowered.

'I thought you were…'

Robbie looks embarrassed.

'We see him outside and we look after him,' said Mrs Afghanistan. There is something in her eyes that tells me that she too has feared for her children's lives.

'Thank you… so much…' I struggle to get the words out.

'He learns very quickly, your son,' said Mr Afghanistan. 'If you like, I teach him to play.' He laughs and adds, 'I think soon he will beat me.'

'Please, please, Mum!'

81

I nod.

I kneel before I get into bed, and pray to whatever created this strange world and the wonderful – and terrible, but mainly wonderful – creatures that inhabit it. I say thank you and promise never to complain about anything or to envy anyone ever again.

'It's like a drug honeymoon,' I say to myself, and fall asleep.

WE'RE NOT BORN HERE

I FRIGHTEN THE WOMEN. They look at the remnants of my beauty and think, 'None of us are safe.' They hurry home to their faithless, bad-tempered husbands, and cling to them in the night. The men linger; some want to save me and others want to piss on me.

When morning rush hour is over, I put four fingers in my mouth and whistle for Argos. He's always across the road, a few doors away. I call him Argos because my father loved Greek and he named my pets after mythological creatures. Argos' brown hair has run wild about his head and his beard is like cloth spun by his chin. I have never heard him speak. I give him money to buy me a bottle of vodka and I add a few pounds for his cider.

I have done well this morning; the spring sun shines rays of hope and commuters dream of eating seafood on terraces by the Mediterranean. I pick up my takings and put them in a secret pocket on the inside of my coat. I take a long swig from a water bottle full of vodka and my body comes to life again, as if I have been touched by a loved one.

I walk to the little square a few streets away and sit on a bench under a plane tree with lime-green bark. Finches are bickering above me and a squirrel stands next to a takeaway box, eating the flesh of an animal ten times his size. Two magpies walk slowly across the grass, like aged actresses. Argos has followed me and he crawls into a clump of bushes on the other side of the square.

Ivor walks towards me with an outstretched hand. He is a tall white-haired man wearing a navy cashmere coat with bald patches.

'Roast beef this morning,' he says, handing me a sand-wich. He gets them from the rubbish bins behind a super-market.

'Thank you, Ivor.'

He sits next to me and we eat our sandwiches. He takes a mouthful of my vodka but he's not a drinker. He was a senior civil servant in the Foreign Office, but his wife came home one day to find he had taken apart every television and radio in the house looking for bugs. He stopped sleep-ing in the same room as her in case she injected him with poison, and he railed at his children for betraying him. He lost everything.

'Has anyone been looking for me?' he asks.

'No.'

He stares at a middle-aged couple standing staring at a statue of Charles II. The man is reading aloud from a book.

'The garden was laid out in 1681...'

'More than three hundred years old and we're standing in it,' says the woman.

'They're tourists, Ivor. Listen – they're American.'

'They have agents in every country.'

84

I notice a newspaper in his coat pocket and say, 'Read to me: tell me what's going on in the world.'

He puts on glasses, one lens cracked like a spider's web.

'The Office of National Statistics has published data on the ages at which people are happiest.'

'What did they find?'

'It seems we're happiest before our mid-twenties and after our mid-fifties.'

'It's when they're free.'

'Why do you say *they*?'

'Because we have resigned our people status.' I take another drink. 'My father believed he would have been happy if he hadn't married my mother.'

'Did they stay together?'

'Unhappiness is more binding than love. My father was a student when he had a one-night stand with a barmaid in a pub car park. I was the consequence of a few minutes' folly. He had to give up his dream of becoming an academic, and she gave up her dream of being loved.'

'It's sad.'

'They got comfort from hurting each other. He was unfaithful and she made his life hell.'

'Would they have been happy if they hadn't married each other?'

'He'd still have been a bastard and she'd have got herself into another kind of mess.'

Colin comes into the square and walks towards us. His upper body is muscular from years of carrying weapons and backpacks. He can't stand still and his eyes scan the buildings behind the square. The wars he fought carry on inside him.

'Anything to eat?' There is threat in his voice.

I shake my head.

He looks at our empty sandwich wrappers.

'Drink?'

I shake my head again.

He spots Argos drinking cider in the bushes.

'Leave him alone,' I say.

I brace myself for a punch.

Ivor quickly pulls pound coins from his pocket and thrusts them at Colin. Colin stares at the money but doesn't reach out to take it. He walks away and leaves the square.

'Thank you,' I say.

'At your service, my lady,' says Ivor, smiling.

I think of his wife and know she must miss the man he once was.

'Mozart lived near here, on Frith Street,' says the American husband. They have moved closer to us.

'So he must have walked this path,' replies his wife. Her dark-blue blazer fits her well and her cream trousers have no creases.

'I guess so.'

'This is why I love London: the past is always present.'

'I'm going to take a photo of the statue. Will you stand next to it?'

The sight of the American's camera has brought terror to Ivor's eyes.

'I have to go,' he says. He stands up and hurries out of the square.

The American has no idea a man has fled from him in fear of his life.

I felt the power of my beauty from an early age. The fathers of my friends would encourage them to bring me on their family outings and holidays, teachers let me away with murder and I was invited to every party.

I wanted to live life, not read about it, so I didn't go to university. I took a secretarial course, where we had classes in deportment and etiquette. My first job was PA to the chief executive of an electronics company. My boss had small eyes, a large nose and the mouth of a monkfish. I tormented him for six months; I opened the buttons of my blouse so he could see my cleavage when I leaned over him to put papers on his desk, I brushed his hand when I gave him coffee and I wore skirts short enough to show my great calves, but not so short I looked like easy picking. I was very formal in my manner so he didn't know where he was.

Our affair started on a business trip and ended three months later when his wife found out. She found out from me – I sent her an anonymous letter. You can make a man tell you anything if you give him the sex he wants, and I had enough information by then about the company money he was siphoning off to his offshore bank account. I suggested I might have a chat with the Serious Fraud Office, and mentioned a large sum that would dissuade me. I expected him to negotiate a reduction, but he gave me the unreasonable sum I'd requested. I spent two years travelling the world and sleeping with beautiful young men with tenderness in their eyes and firm, strong bodies.

'Hello, my queen.'

John-Joe is limping towards me. He's a red-headed giant who broke his body digging the foundations for motorways.

He sits down next to me. 'And how are we this glorious morning?'

'Good, and you?'

'I'm grand. How did you do?'

'Better than usual. The sun, I think. And you?'

'Same. If they're miserable they have no mercy.' He looks around the square. 'Where's Ivor?'

'Fled from a tourist.'

'They're terrifying beasts, all right, with their big shiny white teeth and black sunglasses.'

I offer him some vodka, but he pulls a bottle of Buckfast from his pocket. 'Thanks, I'll stick with the monks.'

I close my eyes, and raise my face to the sun. John-Joe starts singing.

'Oh grey and bleak, by shore and creek, the rugged
     rocks abound,
But sweeter green the grass between than grows on
     Irish ground:
So friendship fond, all else beyond, and love that lives
     always,
Bless each dear home, beside your foam...'

When he finishes, he says: 'I'm thinking of going back.'

'For good?' I ask.

'No. There's a charity that would give me the money for my fare and a few days in a B&B.'

'How long has it been?'

'Over fifty years.'

'It's a long time.'

'Aye.'

'Have you family there?'

'My brothers emigrated, but I don't know if any of the girls stayed behind. I heard all the houses in our area have been bought as holiday homes by Germans and the French. Strangers who know nothing about us sit in our kitchens, sleep in our bedrooms and sow flowers on our farmland, while we're scattered to all corners of the world.'

'Occupied territories. It mightn't be a good idea.'

'Maybe you're right.' He takes another swig from his bottle. 'I'd love to see hares chasing each other around a field on a spring evening. And to wake to the roar of a donkey and a yard full of squawking chickens.'

We sit quietly for a while.

'How long do you think it'll be before Ivor comes back?' asks John-Joe.

'Could be a day, could be weeks.'

'Poor man. He's a true gentleman.'

'He is a gentle man.'

John-Joe looks up at the position of the sun. 'Well, I better go – a funeral down the road in St Pat's.'

'A close friend?'

'A stranger. I like the atmosphere – people come alive in the presence of the dead.'

I laugh.

'I'll see you later, *a stór*.'

'Goodbye, John-Joe.'

I put my feet on the bench and sleep for a while. I dream of the limestone terraces on a Greek island where I once lived.

'Cass, wake up.'

I open an eye to see a young woman with long blond hair, wearing a pale-blue wool coat, leaning over me.

'I'm sorry to wake you, but I want to have a word.'

'You look like a social worker.'

'I'm Margaret's replacement.'

'They never last long.'

I don't like her hovering over me, so I sit up.

'I was wondering if you need anything.'

'No, do you?'

She joins me on the bench, trying to position herself between pigeon droppings. 'It's a nice little square.'

'Have you come to tell me that?'

'I've come to see you because it's not safe for you to—'

'Are you married?'

She looks puzzled. 'No, but I live with my partner.'

'You're at much greater risk of being murdered than I am.'

'Statistically, maybe, but—'

'Statistically, definitely. Remember that when you get home tonight.'

I pass her the vodka, but she shakes her head. I take a long draught. The blackbirds are singing their sweet tunes and the treetops are swaying like drunken dancers.

'It's the toll on your health.'

'You're being paid to sit here and talk to me, aren't you?'

'Yes.'

'I should be paid too. That's something I need.'

'You could die of cold, Cass.'

'I'd be found. My boss only liked blow jobs. Don't stay with a man who only likes blow jobs. What age are you?'

'Twenty-five.'

'You won't be happy again until you're sixty.'

'I'm not sure I believe those surveys.'

'Do you ever look at your partner's face over the cereal bowl and think "That'll be my view every morning for the rest of my life"?'

'We could get you a place quickly because of your age.'

'I have a place – a whole city. *Sans-abri*, that's what the French call us. It means "without shelter". People need shelter from their home. I never had shelter.'

'Do you speak French?'

'We're not born on the streets.' I look at a young couple who have come into the square; they're tangled around each other as if they've just had sex. 'Love is overrated. What do you think?'

'There'll be a van coming around next week to take lung X-rays.'

'Don't get inside his head – you won't like what you find.'

'You're not making it easy for us.'

'I was always searching, searching. It's hard to find something if you don't know what you're looking for.'

'Would you prefer it if I went away?'

'No, I'm enjoying myself.'

It is night and I'm woken by the sound of drunken men.

'Look at this filthy cunt.'

I'm lying on the bench and they're standing over me. One of them holds a lighter to my face and says, 'She looks just like you, Spike.'

'Shut the fuck up.'

'Look at her face – it's your mum, Spike. Jonno, isn't she the spit of him?'

'Yeah, Spike, she is – she's your mum!'

The lighter is taken away from my face.

'Fuck off, you bastards,' says Spike.

I put my feet on the ground and sit up.

'Say hello to your son.'

Someone kicks my legs, hard. I keep very still.

'Say hello to your mum, Spike.'

'I've had enough of this shit.'

'She wants to talk to you.'

'Take her home with you, Spike. You can't leave your mum out here.'

Jonno picks up my bag and pulls out my water bottle. He takes the top off and sniffs, before taking a mouthful.

'It's bloody vodka.' He takes a long drink before passing it to the others. They start to sing:

> 'No one likes us, no one likes us,
> No one likes us, we don't care,
> We are Millwall, from the Den.'

Jonno puts the bottle in his coat pocket.

'See if there's money in the bag – they make loads begging.'

Jonno pulls everything from my bag and scatters the contents on the ground.

'Fuck all.'

The lighter is brought close to my face again.

'Where's your money, you cunt?'

I am outside myself.

'Christ, she stinks. Let's have a bonfire.'

'A barbie. I've never seen a body burn.'

'Save money on a takeaway.'

They laugh.

'We'll need petrol to get a good blaze going. We can tie her to the bench and light the fire under her.'

'There's sticks on the ground and paper in the bins.'

'You been a Boy Scout?'

'Course not, it's common fuckin' sense.'

'Alcohol burns – we could pour vodka on her.'

'She's full of it already.'

'Come on, let's collect paper and sticks.'

They start pulling paper from the rubbish bin nearest to my bench.

'You stupid dickheads, you'd do time for that – a long stretch, at least twenty years,' says Spike.

'How would they know it was us?'

'There's fuckin' cameras everywhere around here.'

They're quiet for a few seconds.

'She needs a wash.'

'Yeah, Spike, your mum needs a wash before you take her home.'

They have started unzipping when I hear the sound of smashing glass. I look towards the sound and see Argos running out of the bushes holding a broken bottle and roaring like a bull. They see the madness in his eyes.

'Jesus, he's a psycho. Let's get out of here.'

Argos waits outside the square until he's sure they've gone. When he comes back, he nods towards me and disappears back into the bushes. I settle down on the bench and go back to sleep.

THE CURRENCY OF LOVE

I WAS GOING TO START AGAIN. There would be no more disastrous love affairs. And I wouldn't choose my friends on the basis of how entertaining they were. I wanted kind people in my life. The software company I worked for offered me a job in London, and I accepted it because I knew no one there. My mistakes wouldn't come banging on my door in the middle of the night. I would listen to Chopin, read Proust and visit galleries.

I found a flat in a pleasant South London suburb. The houses had high ceilings, big windows and long gardens. My flat was on the top floor of a three-storey building, and my bedroom looked out on a flowering magnolia tree.

The evening I moved in I had been staring at the cardboard boxes that contained my life when I heard the buzz of my entry phone. I picked up the receiver and was about to tell the caller they'd pressed the wrong buzzer when I heard, 'Hello, I'm your next-door neighbour. I have something for you.'

It was a woman's voice.

'I've just moved in.'

'I know.'

'OK, I'll come down.'

The first thing I saw when I opened the front door was a small baking dish filled with lasagne.

'I knew you'd be too busy unpacking to cook – I saw you moving in. All you have to do is reheat it in the oven for about twenty minutes, 220 degrees.'

She had black-brown eyes above a long elegant nose, and her head was tilted upwards a little. Her thick brown hair was brushed back from her high forehead, and she had the figure of a Renaissance muse, which was a joy to see in a city where women lived on kale and carrots and used the gym as their place of worship.

'Thank you so much!'

'You're Irish? I love the Irish. I'm Italian – well, born here, but we spoke Italian at home and spent our summers in Italy. I'm Renata.'

'I'm Cara.' I took the baking dish from her. 'This looks delicious.'

'I'll leave you to get on with your unpacking.'

'What's your house number? I'll drop by with the dish tomorrow.'

'Number 42, but there's no rush. You'll have plenty to do.'

When I was back in my flat, I looked at the lasagne and started to sob.

I spent the following day unpacking and trying to rid myself of the desolation felt by all new emigrants. It was about four o'clock by the time I knocked on Renata's door to return the oven dish. She was wearing a yellow silk blouse and a wide skirt with a pattern of pink hydrangeas. There was a boy of about six with a head of black curls on one side of her and a girl, a little younger, with long brown hair on the other.

'The best lasagne I've ever eaten,' I said, holding out the dish.

'Thank you. It's my father's recipe – he's an artist in the kitchen.'

'I'm Sofia and I do ballet,' said the little girl. She stepped in front of her mother and did a pirouette.

'That's wonderful,' I said.

She did another pirouette.

The boy stepped forward. 'I can do eight times tables,' he said, and he rattled it off at great speed. When he was finished, he gave me a gorgeous smile and said, 'I'm Luca.'

The children shone with the special light that comes from being loved and knowing only the good things life has to offer.

'Come in, come in. I was about to make a coffee.'

The internal walls of the house had been knocked down, so the rooms were huge. I sat at a breakfast bar in the kitchen-diner and looked through the open glass doors at the children, who were soaring into the air from their trampoline, while Renata made coffee in a machine that looked more like a piece of sculpture than an appliance.

She served the coffee in fine white china cups.

'Great coffee,' I said.

'My husband's family are Italian too – from Napoli – so we have to have good coffee. There are still only a handful of cafés in London where you can get decent coffee. I sometimes think the English are taste-blind.'

I laughed. 'I'm afraid the Irish aren't any better.'

'Oh, but your oysters and lobsters are fantastic. And your butter... and there's that cheese – Castle Blue?'

'Cashel Blue. Yes, our produce is great, and we're learning not to ruin it. Are you full-time with the kids, Renata, or do you have another job?'

'I studied Fine Art and worked at one of London's top galleries before I had Luca. They're only little for a few years, and I didn't want them being brought up by a stranger, so I decided to give up work for a while. My dream is to have my own gallery. Marco, my husband, is a hedge fund manager, so we didn't need a second income. Don't ask me what a hedge fund is – I lose consciousness whenever he tries to explain. All I know is there aren't any birds in the hedges. What about you?'

'I'm a software engineer. I work mostly from home, which suits me – no office politics, although I do sometimes fall out with myself.'

'Oh, they're the worst arguments,' she said. 'You must come here for coffee breaks. Adult conversations are a treat for me. Marco goes to the gym three evenings a week, so I have whole days when my conversations are limited to the adventures of SpongeBob SquarePants.'

'That would be lovely.'

I dropped in a few days later with a box of cream cakes from a local patisserie.

'Oh, you darling,' said Renata, when she opened the box. 'Marco won't let me buy cakes – he says I'm too fat. I'm afraid you're going to have to fight me for the religieuse and the coffee éclair... and possibly the mille-feuille.'

I had the canelé, and she ate the other three cakes. I don't have a taste for sweetness.

'I'm destroying the evidence,' she said, through a mouthful of cream.

I was soon dropping in about twice a week. One afternoon, when she was walking me to the front door, she said, 'Marco is keen to meet you. Come for supper tonight.'

'OK. Thanks.'

'About eight thirty – the kids will be in bed.'

'Great. Can I bring anything?'

'Absolutely not. Marco is very fussy about wine; he'll only drink certain vintages. He knows more than the sommeliers when we go to a restaurant.'

'I look forward to meeting him,' I said, and wondered when I had learned to lie so well.

Marco opened the door that evening. His short nose was flat at the end, as if its growth had been interrupted, the skin on his cheeks looked sanded – probably a legacy of adolescent acne – and he had his son's black curls. His cobalt-blue suit hung so well it must have been made for him.

'*Benvenuto a casa nostra.*' He kissed me on both cheeks and added, 'Let me take these from you – they're lovely, thank you.' I had brought a bunch of tiger lilies. He led me to the living room at the front of the house. There was a log fire burning in the white marble fireplace and abstract paintings hung from the walls. Renata waved from the kitchen-diner. 'I'll be with you soon – just adding some final touches,' she shouted.

'A glass of champagne?' Marco asked. 'It's a Pol Roger – 2009.'

'Yes, I'd love it.'

He sat opposite me when he returned with the drinks. After we'd tasted the champagne, he said, 'This was Churchill's favourite drink.'

I resisted the temptation to tell him about the murderous thugs Churchill had unleashed on Irish civilians.

'So are you enjoying living here, Cara?' He had the gaze of a boxer eyeing up an opponent before a big fight.

'Yes, it's very peaceful. I love the green spaces, and it's great to have the local cinema and theatre. You have the advantages of a city without too many of the disadvantages.'

'It's a great place to bring up kids – that's why we moved here. Renata told me you're a software engineer. What sort of company do you work for?'

He asked the questions you'd ask a job applicant, and I was relieved when Renata shouted that the meal was ready.

We ate at a long walnut table set with lime-green cloth napkins and cutlery with curved handles and oval spoons. Renata had cooked a casserole, served with polenta.

'It's delicious. What is it?' I asked.

'Ossobuco – veal shanks braised with vegetables, white wine and broth.'

'You're not squeamish about eating calves?' Marco asked.

'Not if I don't know them.' I'd read reports on the conditions under which calves were transported. I started feeling a bit queasy.

'What do you think about the wine, Cara?'

'I'm not very knowledgeable about wine, but it tastes good.'

A fleeting look of distain crossed his face before he said, 'It's from Tuscany. Renata and I visited the vineyard. Do you remember, Renata?'

'Yes, I was heavily pregnant with Luca, and couldn't wait to leave and have a siesta!'

He laughed. 'Cara, if you had money to invest, which software companies would you buy shares in?'

I left at ten thirty – I said I had to be up early to meet a work deadline. I fell asleep worrying if the price of Renata's friendship was going to be evenings with Marco.

I had a text from Renata the following morning: 'Come for lunch.' When she opened the door, she said, 'I want to apologise for Marco. Come in.'

While we were eating her homemade spinach soup, she said, 'Marco isn't very comfortable socially. His father washed dishes in a big London hotel – he had emigrated from a very poor area of Naples and didn't speak good English. And Marco grew up on a council estate in Peckham, the youngest of six children. One of the teachers in his comprehensive school recognised he had a talent for maths and helped him get into Oxford. Oxford gave him great opportunities, but it also made him feel socially inadequate. It didn't help that my parents were against the marriage – my father is an eminent neurosurgeon and my mother comes from an aristocratic Venetian family, and they thought he wasn't good enough. I loved his vulnerability, and I knew he'd be a good father, and he is – the kids adore him.'

'What matters is what he's like with you and the kids.'

'Yes, that is what really counts,' she said. She spoke slowly, as if she was choosing her words carefully. 'But I

sometimes wish he'd stop seeing life as a series of com-
petitions. I don't want my children growing up feeling
they have to win at everything all the time.'

'They'll have other influences in their lives.'

'Yes, they will. It's good to talk to you,' she said, and
she put her hand on mine.

Renata and I continued to meet for coffee, and
sometimes she'd get a babysitter and we'd go to the
cinema or a gallery opening. The only time I'd meet
Marco was when they gave a party or if I bumped
into him on the street, and he was always pleasant and
condescending to me. I would sometimes hear them
shouting at each other, because my bedroom was next
to the wall that joined the two properties, but I didn't
attach any importance to it, because arguing for some
couples is like a sport they play together.

I was finishing work one afternoon when I had a text
from Renata saying: 'Help me hang my new painting.'

She opened the door before I had a chance to press
the buzzer.

'I went to the opening of a new gallery in Battersea
last night and bought a painting I love. Tell me what you
think of it.'

She led me to the living room, where the painting
was on the ground, leaning against a wall. Sofia and
Luca were doing homework at the breakfast bar in the
kitchen and they shouted greetings and waved at me.
The painting was a semi-abstract seascape with swirling
waves in black, blue and white. There were layers and
layers of paint, and the top layer had a rough texture.

'It's great,' I said. 'Seething.'

'That's what I love about it: the energy. The artist dropped it off herself, and she's going to come back later, after she's delivered another painting. She's just the kind of artist I'd like for my gallery when I open it.'

'Where are you going to hang it? There's no room here.'

She nodded towards a painting with blocks of dark red that hung over the fireplace. 'I'm going to take that down and put it in one of the bedrooms.'

After we'd hung both paintings, Renata said, 'Well, I better start cooking. Thanks very much for your help.'

I tried to hide my surprise – I was expecting to be asked to stay for something to eat.

'My pleasure. Talk tomorrow.'

I was walking home after picking up a takeaway pizza a little later when I saw an old red Ford Fiesta pull up outside Renata's house. The car had a few dents on the driver's side and it stood out on a street full of new SUVs. A woman wearing blue overalls splattered in paint got out of the car. Her short blond hair was uncombed and she was wearing men's black work boots. She held a bottle of wine by the neck. Guessing who she was, I went up to her. 'I love your painting,' I said.

She turned her denim-blue eyes on me. 'Cool,' she said, and continued walking to Renata's door.

During the next few months, the red Fiesta appeared on the street more and more often. I was still meeting Renata for coffee, but she seemed distracted a lot of the time, and I didn't stay long. The arguments between her and Marco were getting louder and more frequent. I'd sometimes hear a child crying and the shouting would suddenly stop.

I had a text one afternoon from Renata saying: 'Pasta? 8ish.'

I replied: 'Y'.

It wasn't one of Marco's gym nights, so I was hoping he wouldn't be joining us.

Renata seemed tense, and she spilled a glass of red wine when she was helping herself to the rocket and parmesan salad. After she'd mopped up the wine, she said, 'Marco and I are getting divorced. He's moved out.'

'I'm sorry,' I said. 'It must be very difficult.'

'He wouldn't leave. I've been trying to get him out for weeks. He said I should move out and leave the kids with him, because I was the one who wanted the divorce.'

'What changed his mind?'

'I threatened to have him charged with coercive control. I'd been to a solicitor and I've gathered a file of evidence; he controls all the money, he's stopping me going back to work now the kids are out all day...' She stopped, then went on, 'You don't want to hear all this. I should have left years ago, but I didn't want the kids to suffer.' A convoy of tears moved slowly down her face. 'He'll have them at weekends and he'll ring them every day, so they're not losing him.'

'Is there someone else, for either of you?'

'It's not why we're getting divorced, but I have met someone – Alex, the painter. I didn't tell you about it because I didn't want you to feel... compromised when you met Marco. I didn't want you to feel you were deceiving him. I wanted to keep you clear of the mess.'

'Thank you.'

'I was meeting her to help with her career – giving her my contacts, advising her – because I think she's very talented. And then we fell in love.'

'Does Marco know about her?'

'No. And I don't want him to. I'm sure he's had affairs; I saw nail marks on his back once when I was pregnant. Those gym nights were a good front, and his office is full of beautiful young women. But enough of me – what have you been up to? I want to talk about something else – anything that isn't related to my situation. I'm so sick of it all.'

During the following months, I would sometimes join Renata and Alex for dinner, but I didn't enjoy the evenings. Alex wasn't interested in anything I had to say; she'd look at her phone when I was speaking. And they were constantly touching each other, giving the impression they couldn't wait for me to leave so they could make love. I'd babysit when they wanted to go to the opening of an exhibition or a play. The children were their usual high-spirited selves, and they often talked about outings with their dad. I played computer games with them and we had great fun. I'd become very fond of them. After the children had gone to bed and I was alone downstairs, I always had a feeling of deep unease, as if Marco's ghost was in the room.

I was just settling down to work one Monday morning when I heard screams coming from next door. They were high-pitched to begin with, before deepening into a low primitive animal sound. I grabbed Renata's spare keys, ran down the stairs in my bare feet and out into the street. I got no answer from the buzzer, so I let myself in. Renata was standing in the kitchen-diner, bent over in pain, with her hands on her stomach. There was a mobile phone on the floor in front of her. She was still making the low animal sounds, and staring at the phone.

'What's happened, Renata? What's wrong? Are you ill?'

'He's taken them – my babies! He's taken them. He'll kill them – that's what men do in these situations. Oh, God, he'll kill them! He'll kill my babies!'

I grabbed her shoulders. 'Calm down. You have to tell me exactly what's happened.'

'Oh, Jesus, help me. My babies, my babies.'

She starting sobbing – great heaving sobs that racked her body.

I shook her. 'You have to tell me what happened so I can get help. I'll phone the police.'

She straightened up a little. 'It's too late. He left the country on Friday.'

'How do you know?'

'He texted me a few minutes ago to say he left with them last Friday.'

'He might be lying.'

'He found out about Alex – the kids talked about her – and it drove him crazy. He couldn't bear that she was in his house with his children. I should have known. I should have predicted it. He's a vindictive bastard. Oh, God, I should have protected them. My poor babies!'

'Where do you think he might have gone?'

'Anywhere – he had their passports. He could be in Australia by now. They've never been apart from me for longer than a weekend. They'll be so frightened. Please let them be alive, please, please God.'

'I'm going to ring the police.'

The police came to the house soon after I called; they understood the danger the children were in. There were two of them: a man in his forties and a woman in her twenties. They asked a lot of questions, and told Renata to email them photos of Marco and the children. When Renata mentioned that Marco had found out that she was in a new relationship, I saw the look they gave each other.

'We'll find them,' said the male officer. 'It might take time, but we'll do it. People can't disappear these days.'

'You've got to – before he harms them!' said Renata.

'You did say he's never hurt them in the past...'

'He loves them, but his rage towards me might be stronger than his love for them.'

'Does he still have keys to the house?' asked the woman officer.

'Yes.'

'I think you should have the locks changed – today.'

The house was soon full of relatives. Renata's parents flew over from Italy – they'd gone back to live there after they retired. Her sister travelled from California. And lots of London cousins came to the house every day and cooked for everyone. The Catholic parish priest called around to let Renata know he was going to say a Mass for the safe return of Luca and Sofia – she used to take them to Mass on Sundays.

The police phoned to say they could find no record of Marco having left the country. He hadn't been to work and he hadn't been seen at his flat. Renata told them that two of Marco's brothers were involved with a criminal gang; they'd been to prison, and perhaps they might have been able to get him false passports. The police interviewed the brothers, but couldn't get any information from them. They contacted the *Polizia* in Naples and they interviewed Marco's family there, but his cousins said they hadn't heard from Marco in years. As the days passed, Renata became more and more convinced the children were dead. She was certain they would find a way to contact her if they were alive.

The relatives went back to their lives and Renata was left alone with her grief. The red Fiesta appeared less and less often on the street. Renata looked terrible; she had lost a lot of weight, her hair was unkempt and her skin had developed a yellowish pallor because she never went out in the sun. I called to see her every day, and she was often in her pyjamas late in the afternoon. Each time I saw her, she would grab me by the shoulders and say, 'I should have protected them. That's all I had to do. But I failed them, I failed them.' She would repeat the words over and over again.

She slept in the children's beds so she could smell them on the sheets. When she slept in her own room I would hear her sobbing. I moved to the sofa in my living room because I couldn't bear to hear her pain.

Although Renata was convinced the children were dead, she kept contacting the police to make sure they hadn't stopped searching for them. She wanted to bury her dead children, to have a grave to visit. Her great fear was that Marco had thrown them overboard from a cross-channel ferry. She got money from her parents to hire a private detective, but Marco had cleared his bank accounts before he disappeared, and the detective didn't have any more success than the police. He said the abduction was so well planned, there must have been professional criminals involved. Marco's brothers wouldn't take Renata's calls − they had never liked her. She spent her days on internet sites that helped families find missing relatives.

Nine months after Marco had taken the children, Renata received a text late one night from a mobile number she didn't recognise. Marco's name was at the end of the message and it said he would bring the children to the house the following morning. She phoned me. 'I don't know if it's a trick − it might be someone's idea of a sick joke. A lot of strange people contacted me after the story was in the press. I've no way of knowing the text is from him. If it is, he might be bringing their bodies. Oh, God, please let them be alive. Will you be here when he comes?'

'Of course. But we've got to inform the police. They have to arrest him.'

'I'm worried he'll drive away if he sees police cars.'

'Ask them to come in unmarked cars − I'm sure they would anyway. Marco is a danger to the children as long as he's free.'

'I'll ring them now.'

I got up at 6.30 the following morning and looked out my front window to see if there were any unfamiliar cars. I noticed two black Audi saloons, one parked at either end of the street. I got dressed and went to Renata's house. I knew she wouldn't have slept.

'I'm making you breakfast.'

'I'm not hungry.'

'You have to stay healthy for the children – they'll need you.'

'I don't dare hope… I've pictured them dead so many times.'

She suddenly kneeled on the floor, joined her hands and said, 'Hail Mary, full of Grace, the Lord is with thee; blessed art thou among women…'

'And blessed is the fruit of thy womb, Jesus.' I kneeled beside her and prayed, even though I had long ago stopped believing in her god.

'Holy Mary, Mother of God, pray for us sinners, now and at the hour of our death.'

'Amen.'

She stood up. 'She loved her child. And she couldn't protect him,' she said.

The buzzer went two hours later. I walked to the door and Renata stood some distance back, in the hallway. It took me a second or two to recognise the children – they were wearing supermarket clothes, their hair was badly cut and the light was gone from them. Marco was standing back a little, wearing an old grey tracksuit, and he was in need of a shave. There was a look of satisfaction on his face: Renata had destroyed his happiness and he had destroyed hers.

Marco was convicted of abduction and sent to prison. He had kept Sofia and Luca in an isolated farmhouse about twenty miles from Naples, where he left them locked in a room during the day while he hung out with his cousins in Naples. He told the children their mother didn't want them any more.

Renata lived in fear of losing her children again; she was tormented any time they were away from her. She would drive past their school to see them in the playground or through a classroom window, and she'd go their rooms in the middle of the night.

The children were different after they came back – they would never be the people they would have been. But they were alive, and they were loved. And me – well, I accepted that my life was never going to be a Chopin nocturne.

THE UNCHOSEN

I T WAS A SATURDAY MORNING, and they were lying in bed watching a convoy of dark clouds pass slowly across a mullet-grey sky.

'God, I hate December,' said Andrea.

'It'll soon be the 21st, and we'll start tilting towards the sun again. Did you put the heating on when you were making the coffee?' asked Gillian.

'Yes, but there's frost on the cars, so it'll take a while to warm up.'

Gillian pulled the duvet up to her chin.

'Hey! You're pulling it off me.'

'Sorry.'

She didn't return as much duvet as she'd taken, but Andrea didn't protest.

'We should have two – each of us will have one,' said Gillian.

'Yeah, that's what I was thinking. Who'll have the first one?'

'It should probably be me, because I'm older.'

'What if you have twins? You have twin cousins, don't you?'

'Then we have three.'

Andrea moved closer to Gillian in search of heat.

'Ouch!'

'What?' asked Andrea.

'That's the arm I hurt playing football the other day.'

'They're rough, that new lot you're playing with.'

'Physical, that's what we call it. Or competitive.'

'What'll we do about a dad?'

'A donor. I'm not keen on the idea of a sperm bank –
you don't know what you're getting. They tell everyone
their donor is tall, handsome and intelligent. I'd like to
know them, or at least meet them once.'

'What about asking a friend?'

'Most of our male friends are gay, and most of them
prowl the parks, so God knows what they'd bring to
the party. And the more continent ones have prowler
partners.'

'We could ask your brother.'

Gillian sprung up from the pillows. 'Yuck! That is the
most disgusting thing I have ever heard. Yuck, yuck!'

'For me, not for you! With a turkey baster.'

'I knew what you meant. Nothing of him is going near
you. And I'd be the baby's mother and aunt – too confus-
ing.'

'Lie down! You're letting the cold air in. I think we
should carpet this room – the floorboards look lovely, but
they're so cold in winter. I like a carpeted bedroom.'

'And we'll get flying geese for the wall.'

'You're making fun of me.'

Gillian kissed her. 'I'm teasing you; it's a marital
privilege.'

'So how will we find a donor?'

'There are websites to help women who want to conceive get in touch with donors.'

'Why would any guy want to do it?'

'All sorts of reasons – some altruistic and some narcissistic.'

'And what would we be looking for?'

'A very high IQ, because there's a regression to the mean; bright parents have bright kids, but not as bright as they are, and dim parents have dim kids, but not as dim as they are.'

'What if the baby has learning difficulties?'

'It depends on when we find out.'

'If we didn't know until after the birth?'

'We'll deal with that if it happens.'

Andrea looked out at the desolate sky again. 'I need more coffee.'

'It's my turn, I know, but if you make another one I'll do breakfast.'

'That depends on what's for breakfast.'

'Porridge with cream and whisky, and scrambled eggs with smoked salmon, cheese and fresh chives.'

'Porridge with whisky and cream… it's a deal.'

Andrea got out of bed and pulled on a blue hoodie over her pyjamas.

'Turn up the thermostat when you're down there.'

They were sitting at the kitchen table an hour later, still in their pyjamas. The apple-green cupboard doors and wooden ladder-back chairs gave a rustic feel to the room.

'This is so perfect,' said Andrea, smiling at her porridge.

'The Scots know how to survive this weather.'

'What else should we look for?'

'Good-looking people do better in life.'

'Have you been researching this?'

'I believe in evidence-based living.'

'What evidence did you have for choosing me?'

Gillian leaned across the table and kissed Andrea on the lips. 'I chose you, despite the evidence, because you were very sexy.'

'Despite what evidence?'

'You were drunk.'

'It was my birthday!'

'That's what all the drunks say. We'll have to rule out genetically transmitted diseases like Hutchinson-Gilford progeria.'

'What's that?'

'You get very old very young.'

'I feel it coming on.'

Gillian cleared the porridge bowls and went to the cooker to heat a saucepan for the eggs. Andrea scrolled through her iPod and pressed play when she found Thea Musgrave's *Turbulent Landscapes*. She looked over at Gillian and felt the tug of physical pleasure she always felt at the sight of her long, strong body.

'We've got Jessie's tonight,' said Andrea.

'We should eat beforehand – her food is filthy.'

'She can't help it – she's taste-blind. She thinks she's a great cook.'

'How could anyone who uses a cookbook written for students with recipes for tinned ingredients think she's a good cook?'

'We all have our delusions.'

'She inflicts hers on us.' Gillian poured the egg mix into the saucepan and stirred. 'Turn off that music – it's too ominous.'

'I love how dramatic it is. The composer was inspired by Turner's seascapes.'

'It's too early for drama.'

'It'll be fun to see everyone and have a few drinks.' She turned off the iPod.

'We won't be able to go out much when the babies are born.'

'I suppose one of us could,' said Andrea.

'We're not turning into a straight couple.'

When they were getting dressed Andrea noticed Gillian pulling on a pair of blue jeans. 'You're not wearing your jeans, are you?'

'Yes, why?'

'I was going to wear mine.'

'Can't we both wear them?'

'I hate it when lesbians go around looking like twins.'

'We won't look like twins if we both wear jeans!' said Gillian.

'I'll wear something else.'

'Put on your bloody ballgown.'

'No need to get like that.'

They went back to the kitchen to make a shopping list. Andrea looked around her, and said, 'We'll have to sell the flat.'

'Yes – we'll need two more bedrooms. We'll have to move out a bit.' She opened the fridge to see how much milk was left.

'How far?'

'Putney, maybe.'

'Our friends will be miles away.'

'We'll be too exhausted for friends.'

'Are you trying to put me off the idea?'

'I'm preparing you for the reality. I think my parents will help us buy a place.'

'A reward for acting heteronormative?'

'Grandparents who would like a nice home for their grandchildren.'

'They'll feel they can drop by any time they want.'

'We're going to need all the babysitters we can get,' said Gillian, pulling a phone from her pocket. 'Let's get on with this shopping list.'

Andrea looked out at the vengeful rain pounding against the windowpane. 'I think we should skip the market and go straight to Tesco.'

'OK.'

'If we use the same donor for both babies, they'd be half-sisters or brothers. It would create a stronger bond between them,' said Andrea.

'That's a good idea. We could look into freezing some sperm.' She was checking the wine rack for wine that would kill the taste of the food at the dinner party.

'In our freezer?' asked Andrea.

They both stared at the freezer, full as it was with frozen soups and casseroles.

They were sitting in the coffee shop on the sixth floor of a department store in Sloane Square three months later, waiting to meet a donor.

'Let's have another look at his photo,' said Andrea.

Gillian held out her phone.

'He does look nice. I'm nervous. Are you?'

'No. Maybe we should use rating scales.'

'No.'

'Why not?'

'I think intuition is more important.'

'I could use them and you could rely on your intuition and we'll see if we arrive at the same conclusions.'

'I don't want my child to know she's the product of rating scales.'

'Our child.'

'I want to tell her we chose him because he was a very nice man.'

'I'd like to tell her we did everything we could to give her advantages in life.'

'The human race is not an actual race – we're not on earth to compete with each other.'

'Life on a zero-hours contract, living in insecure accommodation and reliant on an underfunded health service is not the future I want for our children.'

'Maybe people are happy on zero hour contracts – they're free.'

'Poverty is the great enslaver.'

'What do you know about poverty?'

Gillian poured hot milk into her Americano before replying. 'We're doing what women have always done: choosing a mate that will help them have healthy progeny.'

'We should love our child unconditionally.'

'We will.'

'I don't want you engaging them in stimulating exercises as soon as their heads appear during birth.'

'I'm planning on starting way before then: Schoenberg during the conception.'

Andrea had to look at Gillian's face to see if she was joking.

'There he is,' said Andrea. She waved at a very tall man wearing a yellow high-visibility jacket and carrying a cycling helmet. His fair hair was thinning, and he had the physical awkwardness of someone who hadn't been hugged as a child.

'Hi, I'm Paul.' He smiled shyly and pushed his black-framed glasses back up his nose.

'Sit down,' said Gillian, indicating the seat opposite them. 'Thank you for coming. Could we get you a coffee?'

'I'm fine – I don't need anything, thanks.' His voice had no variation in pitch.

'Did you have far to travel?' asked Gillian.

'Seven miles: a nice cycle ride.'

'This is strange, isn't it?' asked Andrea.

'I see it as a job interview. You have a job that needs doing, and I can do it. You must have questions you want to ask me.'

'We'd like to know why you decided to do this,' said Gillian. 'It wouldn't occur to most people to donate sperm to strangers, so you must have a good reason.'

He fidgeted with the strap on his cycling helmet. 'My wife and I divorced before we got round to having children and, as you know, I'm a Professor of Mathematics, and there's a very good medical history on both sides of the family, so it seemed a shame to let good genetic material go to waste.'

'You might meet someone else and have children together,' said Andrea.

'I loved my wife.'

Andrea wanted to put a hand on his, but held back.

'You understand you'll never meet the child if we conceive?' said Gillian.

'Yes, I read the material you sent. I'd like to know if there has been a successful pregnancy, and if it was a girl, that's all. I would have liked a daughter who became a mathematician. A female teacher gave me my love of mathematics, and I'd have named my daughter after her.'

'That's lovely,' said Andrea. 'What was her name?'

'Brunhilda. We were living in Germany – my father was in the army.'

'We'll add it to our list of possible baby names,' said Andrea.

Gillian looked irritated and said, 'We'll let you know if we have a girl. Is there anything you'd like to ask us?'

'It's clear from your professions that you'd be responsible parents, and that's all I needed to know. What other questions do you have?'

'What are you interests outside work?' asked Gillian.

'I play in the London Quiz League.'

'That must be fun,' said Andrea.

'I like it. My team is doing well this year.'

'Anything else?' asked Gillian.

'Space.'

Gillian looked confused.

'I'm interested in anything to do with space exploration. I've been to Cape Canaveral a number of times, and I visited the Russian spaceport in Kazakhstan. I collect artefacts: I have a Teflon pouch used to collect lunar samples and a thermal tile from a shuttle.'

'Would you like to go into space?' asked Andrea.

'Yes, if commercial flights become available in my lifetime, I'd love to. It's my life's dream. I'd volunteer to go to Mars if there was a mission going there.'

'But you'd be away for years – it would take so long to get there and back!'

'I'd like to stay, to help establish a community on Mars. Colonising another planet would be a fascinating experiment.'

'My Daddy is a Martian – it would be a great title for a country and western song,' said Andrea.

He laughed.

'Well, Paul, I think we have all the information we need,' said Gillian. 'It's been lovely to meet you. And we'll be in touch soon to let you know our decision.'

After they had seen his head disappear down the escalator, Gillian said, 'Asperger's.'

'What makes you say that?'

'The flat voice, lack of eye contact and absence of emotion.'

'It's normal male autism. I thought he was sad, especially when he mentioned his ex-wife. He was sweet.'

'A man who is so uncomfortable in this world he wants to escape to another? Let's see what the others are like.'

There was an hour's wait before the next appointment, so they wandered around the furniture department looking at things they might buy when they moved house.

'During my first week at university, a girl at my college asked me what period of furniture we had in my home and I didn't understand the question,' said Andrea.

'She was establishing what caste you came from.'

'She never spoke to me again.'

'You were an untouchable.'

Back in the café, Jerry walked towards them as if they were old friends he was delighted to see again. He had dark, curly hair, and his stomach hung over his beige chinos.

'It's lovely to meet you,' he said, and shook their hands.

'Can we get you a coffee?' asked Gillian.

'Thank you, a latte would be great.'

While Gillian was getting his coffee, he looked of out the floor-to-ceiling window and remarked, 'What a great view! I've never been here before. That's the Albert Hall, isn't it? And there's the Natural History Museum – and I love those red-brick Edwardian mansion blocks; they make you feel there's order in the world. And there's the Carlton Tower. It's the history of London in stone and glass.'

'I love it here. It takes you outside your life,' said Andrea.

'I know what you mean.'

When Gillian came back with the latte, Andrea noticed her staring at Jerry's belly and knew she was wondering if he had the fat gene.

'Why did you decide to do this, Jerry?' asked Gillian.

'My wife and I had a lot of problems conceiving our two children, so we know what it's like to desperately want children and not be able to have them. We decided to help other women who wanted children.'

'You're aware you won't have any contact with the child?'

'Yes, I understand that. I'd prefer not to know if it works – there won't be a birthday or anything to remind me.'

'That makes sense,' said Gillian.

He lifted his coffee mug. 'Great latte.'

'What do you teach, Jerry?'

'History. I teach in a state school, and the parents or grandparents of many of my pupils came from British colonies, so they suddenly become interested when they learn that history is their story. I love it.'

'Did you go straight from university into teaching?' asked Gillian.

'I did my teacher training after my degree.'

He had a small line of bloody full stops on his neck where he had cut himself shaving.

'And how do you spend your time outside work?'

'Anything that'll get our kids away from their screens – hill-walking, visiting National Trust houses, cold-water swimming… They strongly protest, of course, but they will at least have some childhood memories of life outside cyberspace, even if all they remember is blisters, cold and boredom.' He smiled at them, a little sadly.

'Is there anything you'd like to ask us?'

'Will you have only one child?'

'We're planning on having two,' replied Andrea.

'That's good. They'll be able to look after each other when you're gone.'

'That's a nice thought,' said Andrea.

'Anything else?'

'My wife and I decided we won't tell our children we've done this. They'd be very curious about their half-sibling and there's a danger they'd try to find him or her. And it's probably best that you don't tell your child they have a sister and brother.'

'That's fine,' said Gillian.

'And I'd like them to know that my wife and I thought a lot before deciding to do this and that we're doing it in a spirit of love.'

'We'll give them that message,' said Andrea. 'I'm sure they'll appreciate it.'

'What will you do if it doesn't work? Would you adopt?'

Andrea looked at Gillian.

'We haven't discussed it,' said Gillian.

'How soon will you decide if you want me to help you?'

'Very soon. We're keen to get started – we know it might take quite a while.'

'Good. I'll wait to hear from you. I think you'd make very good parents, and I'd like to help.'

They watched him walk in the wrong direction for the escalator, then turn back and wave at them.

'He's lovely,' said Andrea.

Gillian remained silent.

'What's wrong with him? Out with it!'

'He must have got a 2:2.'

Andrea pushed back her chair. 'I don't think I can do this with you.'

'What do you mean?'

'I can't judge people like this – I hate it. I won't meet any more donors.'

She had raised her voice, and an elderly couple at the next table were staring at them, remembering a time when they cared enough to fight.

'How else are we to do it?'

'It's not just how you are with these men, it's how you'll be with my child. I don't want your judgement and… competitiveness anywhere near them.'

Gillian reached out and put her hand on Andrea's arm. 'Calm down; you're not being fair. All I'm trying to do is make our children's lives easier by giving them healthy genes. Straight women don't fantasise about marrying weedy men – they're primed to find powerful, healthy men attractive. We're doing what's natural.'

Andrea pulled her arm away. 'It's not going to stop when they're born – I know you. I don't want their childhood to be a form of combat training.'

'We'll give them all the love and support they'll need, but I also want them to be prepared for a challenging world. What's wrong with that?'

'It's only challenging if you think you have to win at everything. I want my child to play in the park with other kids, to be bored, to fall out of trees, to get in trouble, to grow out of trouble, to have a childhood.'

'Would you like your child to grow up to be like Jerry?'

'I'd be very proud of a son like Jerry.'

'He's mediocre!'

'Most of the human race is mediocre. And I happen to like humans.'

'This is a ridiculous argument.'

'No, it's not. We can't bring up children together if we have such different views on how to do it.'

'We'll arrive at compromises – we always do.'

'I don't want to compromise on what's best for my child.'

'We'll both want what's best for our children. We love each other; we'll love them. Isn't that what really matters?'

Andrea looked out over the rooftops of London. A tear hurried down her face. She knew they would break up if they decided not to have children.

'What could be more important than that?' Gillian spoke softly as if they were lying next to each other. 'We've been happy together, and our children will be happy.'

'I don't think love is enough.'

'How can I prove to you that we can make it work?'

Andrea continued to look out the window as if she was seeing into the future. She was silent for a long time. 'I'll only do it on one condition.'

'What condition?'

'If you agree to go to a sperm bank and take pot luck. We won't state any preferences for intelligence, looks, race or anything else. If you're not willing to do it that way, I won't do it.'

'Why is that so important? It makes no sense.'

'Because our parents would have chosen not to have us.'

THE THING ABOUT
BEING HUMAN

I LIFT A FRAMED PHOTO to dust underneath and Edward says, 'Everyone use to tell me I looked like James Dean. What do you think?' He is sitting in a wheelchair by the floor-to-ceiling window that looks out over the rushing waters of the Thames.

I look at the face – it is cracked like dry earth, and there are oases of white hair on either side of his bald head – and I turn to the photo of a young man in a white T-shirt with hair brushed high above his forehead and a cigarette in the corner of his mouth.

'Yes,' I say. I don't know what James Dean looked like. I saw no films, old or new, when I was growing up; Sarajevo was under siege and my mother was too frightened to let us leave our home. But not even her ferocious love could protect us.

'The photo was taken in Mykonos. My lover was an older man who owned a huge estate in Warwickshire, and he hired a boat that took us around the Greek islands for three weeks. It was before charter flights, and islanders would rush to meet us at the pier when they saw our boat approaching; we were like gods come down from Mount Olympus.'

I have heard this story many times. He talks proudly of a life that my mother and father would have considered shameful – a life that would have brought disgrace to a family.

He points to a photo where he has his arms around another young man with tar-black hair and danger in his eyes.

'That was Jamie; we shared a flat. I was in love in him for years, but I was too white. Our flat was like the UN Headquarters – I met men from countries I didn't know existed.'

The UN failed to protect us year after year as we lay under our beds listening to the shells fall around us and to my mother shouting at God, asking him why he didn't stop the killing.

'Everyone went to the Coleherne: lords and bishops, shop assistants and truckers, doctors and rent boys. We were barely legal, so there was still was that delicious feeling of transgressing. It's all soft furnishings and wedding lists these days.'

He never mentions the third photo – the photo of a young man with kindness in his eyes and a gentle smile – so I know he is the one that mattered.

He shifts his weight in the wheelchair.

'Would you like a cushion?'

'Thank you, Maja. It's my lower back.'

I pick up a cushion from the brown leather sofa and place it against his back. He's still in his blue silk pyjamas and black kimono.

'We danced all night, tried every drug, lived every fantasy and travelled the world. We were free to enjoy all the fruits of the earth. And suddenly the music stopped. It was all over.'

I turn from dusting his computer to ask, 'Have you taken your medication?'

'How can you expect me to remember something like that? Ask me about contract law.'

'I left them by the kettle.'

I wait to see if he'll go to the kitchen, but he stares defiantly at me.

I put down my dusting cloth. 'OK, I go check.'

He makes a face to let me know I have made a grammatical error.

'I will go and check.'

He smiles.

I make him a coffee and give him *vanilice* cookies I baked last night.

'They're addictive. I'll be your dealer and we'll make a fortune,' he says.

'Time for your shower.'

'Christopher Isherwood's uncle used to pay boys not to wash for a month before he had his way with them. Interesting expression: "to have your way with someone". It begs the question of whether you could have someone *else*'s way.'

He tries to shock me, but the part of me that once felt shock died long ago.

'I'm not coming here if you don't shower.'

'All right, all right.'

I wheel him to the wet room next to his bedroom. I bend over and he puts his arms around my neck so I can lift him from the chair. We shuffle into the room like a waltzing old couple, and I lower him into the plastic seat. I help him undress and wash him with the detachable shower head and liquid soap that smells of tangerines.

He lifts his penis and says, 'This has contributed more to the sum of human happiness than any government policy.'

I laugh and he smiles. He has to work hard to get a laugh from me.

I dry him in his bedroom with a towel that's still warm from the heated towel rail.

'What would you like to wear today?'

'I want to look sexy.'

'What you call sexy I might call…'

'OK, manly. Pick manly clothes.'

I search the rails in his walk-in wardrobe and find a green tweed jacket, white shirt and brown corduroy trousers.

'Very retro, but I'll try it.'

When he's dressed, I wheel him back to the window that looks out over the Thames. I give him his *Telegraph* to read, but I know he will spend his time staring at the young men in tight shorts who are cycling along the river path to work.

'I'm going now. Your bean stew is in the fridge. Put it in the microwave for about sixty seconds.'

I make enough food for him when I cook for myself; it's too sad to cook for one person. I charge him for the ingredients only. My mother always cooked enough to feed the many cousins and friends who would call to our home before the war.

'Bean stew again?'

'Do you want to cook for yourself?' He thinks cooking is women's work.

He wrinkles his nose in disgust. 'Am I your favourite client?'

'I read in the newspaper about a carer who poisoned her client. They gave the name of the poison.'

He laughs, as if he approves of the poisoning.

I work for myself. I don't pay taxes because I do not trust the State. I have seen how politicians will let their own people go without food and water so they can buy more weapons. I know how easily a country can fall apart, and I know there is no one to save you when it happens.

I'm on my way to meet a new client in Battersea. I've been waiting a long time for a bus, and I'm worried I will be late. I wasn't given a job once because I was ten minutes late for the interview. English people think punctuality is a measure of a person's worth.

I run from the bus stop and arrive just in time at the three-storey red-brick house. The trees in the street have just been pruned, and the branches look like the stumps of human arms.

The door is opened by a woman in her forties, wearing a dress with pink roses against a white background. Her eyes are cold.

'You must be Maja. I'm Dr Ellison's niece.' She doesn't shake my hand or smile. 'Come inside and meet her.'

She leads me to a long room with oak floorboards and a grey marble fireplace. The alcoves are lined with books, and paintings of the English countryside hang from the walls. There are no photos. A tall, thin woman in her sixties wearing a pale-blue cashmere jumper and loose navy trousers is standing in the centre of the room, leaning on a walking frame.

'Hello, Maja. I'm Elizabeth.' Her smile is warm. 'Georgina and I will tell you about my requirements and ask you a few questions to make sure we're a good match. Is that OK with you?'

'Yes, yes, that's good.'

'Take a seat,' says Georgina, nodding to an armchair next to the fireplace.

'I prefer to stand.'

I don't behave like a servant, and Georgina doesn't like it. I stand with my head held high and look directly into their eyes, because I come from a highly respected family and I'm proud of who I am.

'I need someone to do the general cleaning – dusting, hoovering, cleaning the bathrooms and the kitchen floor. And changing and washing the linen. Georgina comes to stay sometimes for a few days, so you'd have to make up her room. A little ironing would be great, too – I've always loathed it. And there'll be the odd errand: getting a prescription or picking up some shopping I forgot to order.'

'That sounds fine.'

'I can still cook, and I can bathe myself.'

There are lines of pain in her face, and I can see what it must cost her to do these things.

'I would do more to help Aunt Elizabeth, but I live in the Cotswolds and have three sons and a husband to look after,' says Georgina. 'But I'd like a weekly telephone report from whomever we employ.'

'Weekly seems a bit excessive,' says Elizabeth.

'If Mummy were alive it's what she would do.'

'It would be hourly if your mother was alive – she was a terrible fusspot.'

They laugh.

Georgina must be going to inherit the house, and she is here to make sure I'm not the kind of carer who would persuade a vulnerable sick woman to leave everything to me.

'I was thinking of three hours, three times a week,' says Elizabeth.

'Yes, that would suit me.'

Georgina takes a notebook and pen from her bag and asks, 'What qualifications do you have, Maja?'

'I have no paper qualifications. I'm from Sarajevo, and I was a teenager during the siege, so my schooling was disrupted.' I don't tell them that my dream was to become a doctor.

There is a silence. They are wondering if I come from the people who committed genocide or the people who were raped and slaughtered. Suddenly I am the Other. I have lost many potential jobs by telling the truth about who I am.

Elizabeth turns to her niece and says, 'Maja comes highly recommended by a former colleague of mine. She has many years' experience.'

Elizabeth smiles at me as if to say, 'I can handle it.' This woman has a good heart.

Georgina looks irritated by her aunt's comments. 'It's unusual for a carer to work freelance – can you tell us why you don't work for an agency?'

'Many clients prefer to have one carer to help them, and agencies aren't often able to send the same carer for each visit. And I can be flexible about my hours, so if more help is needed one week, I can provide it. And, of course, I charge a lower rate, because there isn't an agency making a big profit. I told Dr Ellison my rates when she telephoned me.' I knew the last point would appeal to Georgina.

'I will need more help in a few months. Would you be able to increase your hours?' asks Elizabeth.

'Yes,' I answer. 'Is there no chance your condition might improve?'

'My aunt has motor neurone disease. She was a very distinguished neurologist, so she is familiar with the course of the disease. She gave her life to public service and now, when she should be enjoying her retirement, she gets this cruel disease.'

'It's not so bad. I get great satisfaction from what I am able to do. You can get used to anything – it's the wonderful and terrible thing about being human.'

She looks at me as if she senses her words would have a special meaning for me.

I start feeling tearful and, at the same time, I'm angry with myself for reacting like this.

'Georgina, will you show Maja around?'

'Yes, of course, Aunt Elizabeth.'

I follow Georgina into a kitchen with pale-green wooden units. The washing machine is an expensive German brand and the coffee machine looks like a computer. The white tiled floor will not be easy to keep clean. We leave the kitchen and climb the wide stairs. I can hear planes flying overhead when we reach the first floor, and I feel my hands beginning to shake; I hide them in my jacket pockets. Elizabeth's bedroom is on the first floor, and it has a large en suite with a bath that must be no use to her now. The sheets on the queen-size bed are made of fine ivory cotton and all the surfaces are clear. She is a woman who likes order.

When we get back downstairs, Elizabeth asks, 'Would you like a coffee, Maja?'

'No, thank you, Dr Ellison.'

'A glass of water or fruit juice?'

'No, thank you. Is there anything else you'd like to ask me?'

'We'd like to see written references – three would be good.' says Georgina.

'That's not a problem,' I reply. I can see she is torn between not liking me and liking my low rates.

'Maja, it's been very nice to meet you, and thank you for coming,' says Elizabeth. 'Georgina and I need to talk, and we'll contact you very soon.'

I'm back in my east London studio flat, in a high-rise block that looks as if it's made of white Lego. I cook and sleep in one bare room with a linoleum floor, but it's warm and clean and everything works; I want nothing that reminds me of the high ceilings, polished wooden floors and marble fireplaces of our home in Sarajevo. I take the bean stew out of the fridge and reheat it.

I watch a programme about vervet monkeys while I eat. Apparently they pay special attention to the calls of older monkeys because the older ones are better at spotting predators and finding new food; the old monkeys are needed.

I have been asleep for hours when I hear my phone
going off.

'Maja, please come. I need your help.'

It's Edward, and it sounds like he might be crying.

'Can't it wait until morning? It's the middle of the night.'

'I need you now. Please come.'

'Have you fallen? Should I call an ambulance?'

'No! No ambulance. I beg you – please, please come. I'll
send an Uber for you.'

He is crying in great heaving gulps, like a child; I have
never heard him like this.

'I'm coming – I'll be there soon.'

'OK.'

The city streets are empty apart from homeless people
sleeping in doorways. The taxi turns down a side street
and nearly runs over a group of young people standing in
the middle of the road with their arms around each other,
singing. I've never done this journey by car, and it's taking
a lot longer than I expected. A tidal wave of panic comes
over me. I should have called an ambulance. If Edward
is having a heart attack, there will be no one to give him
chest compressions. I'm sure that no matter how loudly
you call for help in that apartment block, nobody will
come – the rich don't look out for each other. I see him
lying dead on the floor.

'Hurry! Please hurry,' I say to the driver. 'My friend is
very sick – he might be dying. If you get a speeding ticket,
I'll explain it was a medical emergency. I beg you, please.'

The driver looks at me through the mirror, sees the fear
in my face and presses harder on the accelerator. I start to
feel sick, and open a window in case I throw up.

Edward is lying on the floor beside his wheelchair. His face is covered in blood and one eye is closed. There are two glasses and a half-empty bottle of vodka on the coffee table, next to a metal pipe and a teaspoon. I look again at his bloodied face, and suddenly I am back there.

I had gone out to find something for us to eat; we hadn't eaten in two days. The father of my best friend was selling food on the black market and I had gone to their house to exchange a bracelet of my mother's for whatever he could give us. I had begged my mother to le me be the one to go, because I was longing to see my friend. After I had spent an hour hugging my friend and exchanging news, her father gave me cheese and rice. I was so proud and excited about bringing the food home I ran all the way, forgetting to stay close to buildings to avoid being shot by snipers. When I got to our street, all that was left of our home was smoking rubble. At first I thought I had taken a wrong turning and was on some other street, but our neighbours' homes were on either side of the rubble. I walked slowly to the gap where our front door had been. I saw my mother's bloodied head lying in a fireplace; I recognised her earrings. My sister's arm was hanging from a cupboard door, and my father's body was on fire.

'Maja, Maja, don't just stand there, help me up! Maja, Maja!' Edward is shouting at me.

'Oh, God,' I say. 'I think we should get you to a hospital.'

'No! No, I won't go.'

I help him get back on his chair. I struggle to lift him, because my body is shaking and the strength has left my arms.

'I'll clean the wounds and see how bad they are.'

I get a bowl of water, a clean cloth and a tube of disinfectant. I touch him lightly, but he still winces in pain. When I have washed away the blood, he says: 'I won on points.'

I look closely at the cuts. 'You might have scars if you don't get stitches.'

'Excellent – James Dean after the car crash.'

'You could have been killed. If you'd hit your head...'

He looks towards the door and says, 'Will you stay the night? I'll pay you.' There is fear in his eyes.

I nod.

I wheel him into his bedroom, help him put on his pyjamas and get him into bed. I bring a glass of water and two painkillers. I check the locks on the front door and leave the key in the mortise lock in case someone has copied a key. I make up the cold spare room – he has the radiator turned off – and get into bed in my clothes.

I lie in the darkness with my eyes open, because I see my mother's head when I close them. Edward won't pay me for staying the night; he'll pretend he has forgotten. He often tells me he has run out of change so that he can give me a few pounds less than the wages we agreed on. He is rich, but he gets some sort of pleasure from cheating others. We will fight about how much he owes me, but we will make up – we always do, because we only have each other.

YES, SHE SAID

I LOVED THEIR PARTIES; it wasn't just the setting – a Victorian house in Chelsea with high ceilings and long windows overlooking the river – or the food, which was prepared by a professional chef, or the carefully chosen wine: the parties were great because the sisters weren't tribal. They had been born and expensively educated in England, as had their parents, but they were as Greek as their sailor grandfather, who had married well and used his bride's money to create a successful business sending container ships around the world.

A composer friend took me to the first party. We arrived at about eight on a Monday evening, and we had to turn sideways to get past all the guests chatting in the hallway. The crowded living room was furnished with a Knole sofa upholstered in burgundy velvet, a chaise longue covered in green silk and bleached wooden chairs. Terracotta olive jars served as lamp bases. The walls were covered in paintings – nineteenth century landscapes next to expressionist abstracts – and piles of books were scattered around the floor.

The dining room opened into a garden with an ancient oak tree that raised its twisted arms to the heavens, and wild flowers created an illusion of a meadow. The chef stood behind a long mosaic dining table, serving baked sea bass and roast lamb. A waiter with a blond pony-tail and a white jacket with epaulettes was offering us glasses of pink champagne when Sofia rushed up and embraced us.

'I'm so glad you could come!' She was small and slight, her dark hair was dense and curly, and her eyes were the colour of Metaxa. The beads around her neck were Mediterranean blue, and her long yellow skirt had red and green stripes.

She turned to me. 'Rachel told me you're a writer. Are you a poet? I do love poetry. I read Emily Dickenson every morning:

'What fortitude the soul contains
That it can so endure
The accent of a coming foot,
The opening of a door.

'But I'm sure you're just as good. You must let me read your work.' Her upper-class English accent was at odds with everything else about her.

'I write poems that no one reads.'

'You're a real writer!'

'That's a kind interpretation, but would you call a homeowner who unblocks his drain a plumber?'

'Do you write every day?'

'Most days.'

'The homeowner doesn't unblock his drain every day.'

'And I unblock drains that aren't blocked.'

142

She laughed. 'Let's meet for coffee – bring your poems. We could have a reading here some evening; Elena and I often invite our friends to read or perform their work. A cellist played one of Rachel's compositions once.'

'Yes, it was very helpful. I set fire to the score when I got home,' chimed in Rachel.

'You never told me that!'

'It was the only thing to do. I needed to hear it as a listener – I'd got lost inside it.'

'Art isn't for the faint-hearted, is it?' asked Sofia.

'Life isn't for the faint-hearted. We should abandon the concept of art,' I said. 'People create stuff, and other people like it or are moved by it, but there's no need to sanctify what's created by calling it art.'

'I'd love to discuss this further, but I've just seen Father Papageorgiou's about to leave, and I must talk to him.' She nodded towards a priest in a black cassock with a long beard that divided in two, as if it had fallen out with itself. 'We'll talk about the concept of art when we meet for coffee.'

Rachel and I stood by the black marble fireplace with our drinks. I wanted to discuss Sofia, but was worried I'd be overheard. A young guy with a shaved head wearing blue workmen's overalls and army boots stood near us. He was staring in our direction, as if daring us to speak to him.

'Hello, I'm Rachel.' She held out her hand to him. Rachel has long auburn hair and eyes the colour of wild ferns.

'Nick,' he said, ignoring the outstretched hand. 'Do you think he'd give me a doggy bag?' He nodded towards the chef.

143

'I'm sure he would – there'll be plenty of food left over,' said Rachel. 'What breed of dog?'

He started barking and handed us each a card he took from his overalls.

'What kind of installations?' I asked, having read the card.

'I smash things, I find the part that's central to the working of the object and I display that.' He took out a photo of a highly polished piece of steel on a varnished wooden base.

'It's… beautiful,' I said.

He smiled, and suddenly looked like a sweet little boy.

'It's from a washing machine. Come to my exhibition.'

'Are you trying to do more than create lovely objects?' asked Rachel.

'I'm an anarchist. We want to show what's going on behind society – we'll take it apart and not put it back together.'

'I don't think women would fare very well under anarchy,' I said.

'Patriarchal capitalism hasn't done you much good.'

'We're slowly seeing legislation that protects and empowers us,' I replied.

'Why wait? We only have now. Join us and create the kind of society you want to live in. Come with me to our next meeting.'

'What does your group do?' I asked.

'You'll have to come to a meeting to find out.'

'I hate secrecy and clubs.'

'Bourgeois feminists don't want anything to change. You don't give a damn about your working-class and black sisters.'

'I live in a squat, I don't drive car and I own nothing other than a case of clothes and some books, so I'd hardly call myself bourgeois,' I bit back.

'A working-class woman would never live in a squat; she has no safety net.'

'It's good to meet a man who can explain to me what a bad feminist I am.'

'Cheers, sister,' he said, and walked over to the chef to ask for his doggy bag.

Elena, Sofia's sister, joined us, and Rachel introduced me. Elena had the features of an aristocratic Athenian from the classical period, but her beauty was marred by a permanent expression of apprehension; she looked as if some great catastrophe was about to befall the world.

'Have you seen Sofia? I need to talk to her immediately.'

'She went off to speak to Father Somebody-or-Other.'

'He'll be trying to get money for his roof. If his parishioners got half as much attention as his beloved church, his services would be better attended. We're running out of soft drinks; I must find her.'

'How is the painting?' asked Rachel.

'Turn around.'

We both turned to look at a semi-abstract oil painting of a woman standing alone in a rocky landscape under a bank of black clouds.

'Self portrait?' asked Rachel.

'Very perceptive of you.'

'It's powerful,' I said.

'Thank you. I must go.'

After she'd had moved away, I muttered to Rachel, 'An interesting family.'

'Yes, I often worry about what will become of them.'

'Why?'

'They have a kind of innocence – their wealth has protected them.' She looked over at the small queue that was gathering at the food table. 'Come on, let's eat.'

A tall, fair-haired man wearing white jeans and loafers started chatting to me in the queue. 'That gentleman over there told me I was scum,' he said. He was nodding towards the anarchist.

'Why?' I asked.

'I work in financial services.'

'I don't know what that means.'

'I invest rich people's money so they can become richer. It's gambling, with little risk to me.'

'It sounds like fun,' I said.

'It is,' he said, looking surprised. 'But it isn't very laudable, is it?'

'I've given up judging people,' I replied.

'Are you missing it?' he asked.

'Condemning others is one of life's great pleasures; I can't wait to get back to it.'

'The only thing I was good at in school was maths.'

'Don't let him rattle you. He told me I'm a bad feminist.'

'Ouch. What did you do to warrant that?'

'It's what I haven't done.'

Our plates were full and we'd arrived at the end of the table. He looked down at his lamb. 'This is for my wife; she's with the kids next door – I have to take it out to her. We're doing two-hour shifts and she was afraid the food would be gone by the time she got here.'

'Warn her about the anarchist,' I said.

'He's just her type – she'll probably go home with him.'

I had another look at the anarchist, and realised he was rather attractive when you didn't have to listen to him.

Rachel and I took our food out to the garden. A man with wild white hair and a face that looked as if it had been roughly grated was drinking a bottle of beer at a wooden table. He was wearing a dirty grey anorak, and I wondered if he was the gardener. I was sure I'd seen him before somewhere.

'Do you mind if we join you?' Rachel asked.

'No,' he answered, and moved to make room.

'I like it here – it's peaceful,' he said.

His accent was east London, and his voice suggested he was younger than he looked.

'Have you eaten?' I asked, looking down at my sea bass. 'The food is great.'

'The girls always put on a good spread.'

'Have you known them long?' I asked.

'Years. Sofia brings me a coffee most mornings, and if they've any dinner left over they bring me up a plate.'

I suddenly remembered where I'd seen him before.

'I saw you outside M&S one morning – I was impressed by how neat a roll you'd made of your sleeping bag.'

He smiled. 'I was in the navy.'

'That must have been interesting,' said Rachel.

'Our ship was bombed in the Falklands. We listened to the screams of our friends who were burning while we got away in our lifeboats.'

'I'm so sorry,' said Rachel.

'We were heroes when we sailed into the Solent mist that April morning. We were going to fight for our country

147

and save our people. Thousands lined the port; people were willing to lose a day's pay to see us off. We stood shoulder to shoulder on deck. It was the happiest I've ever been. The man on my left never came back, and the one on my right lost half his face.'

'But you did what you set out to do,' said Rachel.

He looked as though he had vacated his body. 'We had only seen war in films.' He was silent for a while.

'Are you OK?' I asked.

He looked confused for a second. 'Yes.'

'Are you sure?'

'Yes. Yes, I am.'

'Would you like me to get you a drink?' His beer bottle was empty.

He looked towards the sun, which was disappearing behind the oak tree, and said, 'I have to go, or my pitch will be taken.' He rose slowly, as if his body was protesting about having to move.

'I'll drop by with a coffee some time,' I said.

'Milk and two sugars. Enjoy your evening, ladies.'

Sofia phoned me the following morning, and we arranged to meet for lunch a few days later in a Greek restaurant called the Epicurean. She rushed up to my table. 'I'm so sorry I'm late – I've just been to a wonderful exhibition, Alice Neel at the Whitechapel, and I couldn't tear myself away. You know an artist is great when you can't bear to leave their company. What are you doing tonight? I've got a ticket for *The Rite of Spring*. Have you brought your poems? Oh, what shall we eat?'

She spoke Greek to the waiter, who knew her well, and she persuaded him to bring us lots of taster dishes, because she wanted me to try everything. She chose wine from a monastery on Mount Athos. She read my poems and said she loved them, which is the only literary criticism any writer wants to hear.

'So who did you talk to at our party?'

'I met your friend from M&S.'

'Colin? He's such a sweet man. He couldn't work after the Falklands, and his wife left with the children. He lost everything. He stayed with us for a few nights when it was snowing last winter – you can't leave a man to freeze to death a few yards from your warm house, can you?'

I thought of the many freezing nights on which I had walked past homeless people lying in the street without giving them a thought.

'His sheet and duvet cover were missing after he left, and we thought he must have taken them by mistake, but he brought them back the following day, washed and ironed. He'd taken them to a laundry. Who else did you meet?'

'Your neighbour who manages investment funds.'

'They've had to put up with Druids chanting and dancing at dawn in the garden, anarchist friends playing heavy metal at full volume, a puppy that barked all night and took chunks out of their children and God knows what else, but they never complain. Did you meet Jake, the installation artist?'

We talked until it was time for her to go to Sadler's Wells. I went with her to the Underground, and as I watched her walk down the station steps, I felt as if I had been swept up in rapids all afternoon, and I was finally getting back on the riverbank.

We started meeting regularly. We'd go to a play, a film or a concert – she had to see everything – and have a coffee or a drink afterwards. I was working in bars at night, so we'd usually meet in the afternoons. She always wanted to discuss whatever we'd seen, and she would have strong opinions about it. We'd been to a film one afternoon about a woman who was murdered by the South African police because she was an anti-apartheid activist. Sofia was silent when we went for a coffee afterwards, so I asked, 'Is there something wrong?'

'I feel so useless. My life is pointless. It's ridiculous. I'm ridiculous.'

I was shocked by the despair in her eyes.

'You always seem so… alive.'

'It's distraction. I keep busy to avoid the emptiness, the desolation.'

I struggled to find words that might help.

'Does everyone have to be useful?'

'I think we need to feel… purposeful – even if it has no basis in reality.'

'You live creatively; doesn't that give meaning to your life?'

She picked up her bag. 'I've got to go. I'm not fit for human company when I'm feeling like this.'

'Wait and finish your coffee, at least.'

'No, you wouldn't thank me if I stayed. I'd infect you.'

She was gone before I could reply. I lay awake for a long time that night, going over the conversation and again and again, and feeling troubled.

We met to see a play a few weeks later, and she was her usual self again. She said nothing about the previous meeting. It was as though an imposter had taken her place – an imposter about whom she knew nothing.

Rachel invited us both to a dinner party a week later. We were seated at opposite ends of the table because Rachel liked to place her guests next to people they didn't know. The man sitting opposite me was about six foot four and had a gaunt face with a long nose and cold eyes. Rachel had mentioned he was her cousin, and that he had just come back from living for many years in Chicago. He didn't address a word to me for fifteen minutes – I clearly wasn't pretty or elegant enough, or failed to meet some other criterion he used to determine who was worthy of his attention. I leaned forwards and said, 'Harrison, I hear you've been living in Chicago. How was that?'

'The theatres have the most sophisticated equipment you'll find anywhere in the world, so in many ways it was excellent.'

His voice was a deep baritone, and he spoke as though he was addressing a crowded room.

'Rachel didn't mention you were an actor.'

'I'm a heart surgeon,' he said, looking around for someone to rescue him.

I wasn't going to let him escape me. 'Not many Americans can access the best quality treatment.'

He launched into a monologue on the economics of health care that lasted from the starter to the pudding. His voice was so loud it was impossible for the other guests to continue with their conversations. He didn't stop until

151

Rachel interrupted him. 'Harrison, this is all very inter-esting, but we've had enough. You're not talking to your medical students.'

He started blinking, and for a horrible moment I thought he was going to cry, but his eyes went cold again.

'I think we should toast the hostess, to thank her for the excellent food,' said the charming man sitting next to me.

'Was it all right?' asked Rachel.

'Delicious,' I said.

'The fish pie could have done with a little more chilli, but otherwise excellent,' said Harrison.

I got up and went to talk to Sofia – I'd had enough of him and his dead-fish eyes.

'I'm going to leave soon, Sofia,' I said. 'I don't want to miss the last tube. Do you want to come with me?'

'I'll wait a bit longer and get a cab. I could drop you off?'

'No, thanks – I'm tired.'

'If you're sure. Let's talk in the morning.'

'Good.'

Rachel saw me to the door, and whispered, 'Apologies about Harrison – his American wife left him and took the children, so he's in a bit of a state. He's hopeless on his own. I promised my mother I'd keep an eye on him.'

'An ear might be more useful.'

Sofia was on the phone at seven the following morning.

'Sorry to phone so early, but I have to talk to someone.'

'Is there something wrong?' I sat up and leaned against the wall; my mattress was on the floor.

'No – something very right; I've met someone.'

A cold feeling surged through me.

'That's fantastic!' I said. 'Who is he?'

'You met him last night – you were sitting opposite him.'

'The surgeon?'

'Yes, isn't he wonderful? We talked and talked until Rachel threw us out, and then we came back here.'

'Did you do the wild thing?'

'Yes, he's just left. He's such a good lover – it must be his knowledge of anatomy.'

'People don't usually require maps.'

She laughed.

'It feels so right – I feel I've come home. He's brilliant, and you know how sexy I find that.'

'Don't rush into anything. Remember what Yeats said: "She bid me take love easy… but I was young and foolish, and now am full of tears."'

'I prefer Molly Bloom's "and yes I said yes I will Yes."'

'Oh, God,' I said. 'There's no rowing back if you're in those waters.'

They got married a few months later in a registry office in the King's Road. Harrison didn't want a big wedding, because he'd done all that last time. Elena, who referred to her future brother-in-law as Bluebeard, wore a shade of navy that was indistinguishable from black, and the groom's family were subdued because they thought it far too soon for him to remarry. Colin borrowed a ceremonial uniform from an old friend who was still in the navy, and he had his hair cut short; he looked very distinguished.

They bought an Arts and Crafts house with a large garden in Kent. It was miles from public transport, and Sofia didn't drive, so her trips to central London became less and less frequent. About a year after they moved into the house, she invited me to a garden party.

I arrived early and I wandered around the garden while Sofia did some last-minute food preparations. The plants were clipped into geometric shapes, the flowers stood to attention in orderly rows and there wasn't a daisy to be seen on the shorn lawn. I looked up at the house and saw Harrison staring at me from a first-floor window. He didn't look away when he knew I'd seen him.

Sofia introduced me to the other guests as they arrived. Most of them were hospital staff who worked with Harrison, and you could feel his power as their sentences tailed off and they turned from the person they were speaking to when he approached them. A few of Sofia's old friends arrived, and we huddled together like birds that had flown off course.

I was passing the kitchen door on my way to the bathroom when I heard a raised voice. I stopped just past the door so I wouldn't be seen.

Harrison was shouting, 'I told you there were six vegetarians. What's wrong with you?'

'I forgot – it went clean out of my head. I'm sorry.' Sofia was talking in that exaggeratedly calm way you do when you're trying to modulate someone else's emotions.

'We've invited them to our home – we have to feed them!'

'I'll find something in the fridge; I'll concoct something.'

'They're hungry now. If they don't eat they'll get drunk, and that's not the kind of party I want this to turn into.'

'I'll be quick. Just let me get on with it.'

'What's in the fridge?'

'I don't bloody know!' she screamed.

I couldn't bear to hear any more.

We lost touch, but I often found myself thinking about her and feeling guilty. I'd tell myself she was an adult woman who was free to make her own choices. But I couldn't rid myself of a lingering feeling of unease. If I saw someone in the street with similar hair or who resembled her in some way, I'd rush up to get a good look at them, and walk away feeling disappointed. I asked mutual friends and acquaintances about her, but they never had any news, which didn't seem like a good sign. Someone told me Elena had gone to live and paint in Crete. I passed their house one day, and noticed the hollyhocks at the front were wilting. I had a dream about a Minotaur that night.

I was leaving a theatre one evening some years later when I saw Sofia in the foyer, standing in a little group. I rushed up to her.

'How lovely to see you!' she said, and hugged me. 'We must meet. Are you free for breakfast tomorrow?'

'Yes,' I said.

'Marcello's, eight o'clock.'

I assumed she must be spending the night in London.

'Great.'

Marcello's was an Italian ice-cream parlour on Wandsworth Road that served great coffee. We'd met there a few times before on a Saturday morning to read the papers.

'Sorry I'm late. I went to see the cygnets in the park; they're so adorable. How are you?'

Her face had lost the roundness of youth, and I realised we were both getting old.

'I'm good. I've got a job as commissioning editor for a publisher, so I have the pleasure of stopping other poets being published.'

She laughed.

'How are you?' I asked.

'Well, I've left Harrison.'

She saw the look of relief on my face.

'It wasn't like that. I was very happy with him, and that's what I couldn't stand. We had an occasional row, like any other couple, but we loved each other and we got on incredibly well. We had a lovely life. But I hated waking up to the same face every morning, even though it was the face of someone I loved. I hated waking and knowing what I was going to do that day. I disliked the smugness of being happy, and the sameness of it. I missed... feelings. I am a creature who likes to surf the waves, and I was on the shore looking longingly at the turbulent seas.'

'How did Harrison take it?'

'Badly. He's convinced there's someone else.'

'Is there?'

'I left him for myself.' She tasted her double espresso. 'God, I missed good coffee!'

'When did you move out?'

'Six months ago. It was awful; he was howling.'

'Do you miss him?'

'Yes, of course. But I also enjoy that. Do you think that's perverse?'

'No.'

'I'm sure I'll end up old, ill and alone, but I will have lived my life, and not retreated into the bunker of marriage. I tried happiness and found it wanting. I don't think humans have evolved to be happy. We enjoy conflict, we like deprivation followed by satiation, we like to love and lose and love again, we relish the relief we feel when pain stops, we like feeling safe after we've known fear, we enjoy feeling rage and we like to forgive. Happy marriages are anaesthetising.' She looked at me above her raised coffee cup. 'Now, tell me about you. Are you in love?'

We talked and talked until it was time for her to leave for her bee-keeping course. After she'd gone I sat for a long time, feeling a bit bewildered.

THE EXISTENTIALIST AND
THE MINESTRONE

K IT'S MOBILE RINGS at exactly 2 p.m.
    'Why does everyone schedule a time to ring?'

'It gives a structure to the day,' says Sarah.

'The day mightn't want structure.'

A robin crashes against the bay window in Kit's first-floor living room.

'Ouch,' she says.

'What?'

'It's the robin who flies into my window. I try to frighten him away, but he keeps on smashing into it.'

'I know how he feels; it reminds me of my first marriage,' says Sarah, laughing. 'It creates an illusion of control.'

'What does?'

'Booking in times to ring people. How are you?'

'I miss the planes.'

'Why?'

'They drowned out the birds, and now I'm woken by the dawn chorus at 4.30,' says Kit.

'I can't believe you can sleep through planes but not birdsong!'

'The birds all sing different tunes – it's a mess; the noise from the planes is continuous and low pitched. And I miss cars.'

'I suppose you like the scent of air pollution?'

'I love to see police speeding to the scene of a crime, plumbers hurrying to fix a leak, pink and white vans bringing flowers to a lover… I love busyness,' says Kit.

'I'm enjoying the quiet – I feel like I'm living in a village.'

'You could have moved to the country.'

'"Could have" – we talk as if there isn't a future,' says Sarah.

Kit hears wheels on the footpath under her window.

'It's the postman,' she says. She opens the window and waves.

He holds up a white envelope and shouts: 'Premium bonds.'

'It's never move than twenty-five.'

He puts both hands on the envelope as if he's about to tear it in two.

'No!' shouts Kit.

He laughs, slides the envelope through the letter box and calls, 'See you tomorrow.'

She watches his broad red back move slowly down the empty street.

'He's friendly,' says Sarah.

'He looks like a monkfish.'

'I've only seen them beheaded, covered in sauce.'

'The vegetables would jump from the plate if the head was left on.'

'We might die,' says Sarah. 'But we probably won't.'

'That's what they thought.'

'Who?'

'The dead ones.'

'I suppose it was.'

Kit starts walking in circles around her living room. 'I'm getting images from the past,' she says.

'What sort of images?'

'I was standing on a stone bridge in a medieval town with my mother. I should warn you – I'm going to cry while I tell you this.'

'That's OK.'

'My mother turned to me and asked, "Will you think of me when I'm gone?" I felt a surge of rage. I was thinking, "She's trying to control what happens after her death." I looked away from her and didn't answer. It would have cost me so little to say "Of course I will!" or "I love you, Mum."' She starts sobbing. Sarah doesn't say anything. 'And I think about her all the time, because I didn't say those things. Why wasn't I big enough? She was asking so little of me.'

'We're all fuckwits.'

'I knew at the time what I should have said. But I couldn't move beyond the rage. She never asked again. The hurt was too deep.'

Kit's hand is wet with tears.

'You were there with her. That's what really matters.'

'It wasn't enough.'

'She might not have attached any importance to it.'

161

'I know her… knew her.'

'We all do it: fail the people we love.'

'It was such a small thing at the time, but it's all I remember now.'

There is a silence before Sarah says, '*Ego te absolvo a peccatis tuis in nomine Patris et Filii et Spiritus Sancti.*'

'Where did you get that?'

'I've been reading Graham Green, and I did A level Latin. I've always envied you Catholics the confession. It must be so… exhilarating to be forgiven.'

Kit sits in an armchair by a fireplace with an empty grate. 'You had to be seen to go into the box and come out again quickly. If you were there for longer than a few minutes, everyone would think you were pregnant.' She dries her wet hand with her T-shirt. 'Have you been haunted by anything?'

'I had an abortion.'

'You never told me!'

'It was before I met you. She'd be thirty.'

'They told you it was a girl?'

'I always knew if I was carrying a girl or a boy. I have a clear picture of what she would look like: she'd have auburn hair and kale-green eyes. She'd be musical and would have studied at the Royal College of Music and become a composer.'

'You think about her a lot?'

'Lately, yes.'

'Does Ben know about her?'

'No – I kept her separate from my family. It was long before I met him.'

'Is he in the house now?'

'He's gone out to see if he can find eggs. I would have been one of those mothers who can't comfort their crying child because they feel the mother's cold anger; a mother trapped in a life that's crushing her.'

'You weren't that kind of mother.'

'I wasn't.'

Kit looks over at the brass candlesticks covered in red wax on her dining-room table. She remembers an evening of good-tempered arguing, gossip and flirting. The candles are burned down to the sticks.

'What else comes back to you?' asks Sarah.

'I was at a party one night, a long time ago, and someone I had been talking to earlier came up and asked if they could drive me home. My life would have been very different if I had said yes. And that moment, when I said no, has been coming back to me, again and again.'

'How would your life have been different?'

'It would have been… safe. Not boring – it would have been full of good things: art, travel, interesting people. And I would have been loved.'

'Why did you say no?'

'I suppose it wasn't what I wanted. I'd just discovered existentialism, and I had a heightened sense of how absurd life is. I used to quote Camus, who believed that life is absurd due to the incompatibility between human beings and the world they inhabit. I knew the next morning that I would never again be offered that kind of happiness. I understood what I had given up.'

'Maybe you could meet again?'

'Someone else is living the life I could have had. I hear about them sometimes.'

'I think everyone has someone like that. Are you still an existentialist?'

'Sort of. It's more a rejection of other philosophies and religions than a well-developed system of thought. It's applied atheism. Existentialists believe that the only meaning life has is the meaning each individual ascribes to it.'

'It's a bit chilling.'

'That's existential angst. What would you call yourself?'

'I'm more of a minestrone – a bit of humanism, some Buddhism and a little Jainism with some Quaker seasoning.'

'How do you integrate it all?'

'I don't,' answered Sarah, laughing. 'It's a minestrone, like I said: lots of little bits floating about.'

Kit hears a siren and she hurries to the window. 'Can you hear that?'

'Yes. It's very near you.'

An ambulance turns into Kit's road, speeds past her window and pulls up at the end of the street.

'It's stopped,' says Sarah.

'Oh, God – I know the woman who lives in that house; she walks her dog in the park.'

Two figures wearing white protective suits and blue masks jump from the ambulance and run into the house.

'I won't look,' says Kit. 'She deserves her dignity.'

'Are you OK?' asks Sarah.

'Yes.'

Kit looks around the room, seeking comfort from the permanence of objects.

'She might recover,' says Sarah.

'Tell me something else that's coming back to you.' Kit sits down again by the empty grate.

'There was a time when everything about Ben drove me into a frenzy of irritation,' says Sarah. 'The noises he made when he was eating, his cheerfulness in the morning, the sound of his voice, his huge feet, the smell of his breath, the noisy games he played with the children, the sound of him peeing. Everything was unbearable.'

'Did he know?'

'He knew something was wrong. I was trying so hard to control it – I was like a wound-up toy.'

'When was this?'

'The kids were small.'

'How did you get out of it?'

'I decided I would treat him with the kindness I'd show a stranger. I got up every morning and behaved as if he was a guest in my house.'

'And that got you through?'

'It took a long time, but yes.'

'I don't think I could do that. I'd feel I wasn't living authentically.'

'It wasn't just about me. Freedom is the price you pay for love.'

'It's a high price.'

'It is. But freedom doesn't hold you in the night when you're frightened.'

'The siren's started up again,' says Kit.

'I can hear it. They got her out quickly.'

Kit starts circling the room again. 'Sarah…'

'Yes?'

'I met her in the park about a week ago. We chatted.'

'Did she seem ill?'

'No.'

'Did you stand near her?'

'I don't think so.'

'You'll be fine.'

'I wouldn't mind pain, or being dead. It's just such a lonely way to go.'

'You won't be alone.'

'Everyone is alone amongst strangers.'

'She mightn't have had it when you met her.'

'If I'd left home five minutes earlier I'd have missed her. It's luck if you get it, and luck if you survive.'

'I can't bear to think it's so random.'

'The world is indifferent to us. It was luck you met Ben, luck you had healthy children.'

Sarah lets out a deep breath. 'That's why we must care for each other.'

'You've scheduled another call, haven't you?' Kit starts picking at the wax on a candlestick.

'It doesn't matter. They can wait.'

'Who is it?'

'Alison.'

'She'll contact the emergency services if you're a second late ringing her. She puts on a mask to phone people.'

'I don't want to leave you.'

'I have to find out how much I won in the premium bonds. Maybe I'm on a lucky streak.'

'I can stay on the phone while you go down to get the letter.'

'I'll be OK.'

'Are you sure? I can ring Alison and tell her I'll talk to her later.'

'Yes, I am. Sarah, I want you to know… that I love you.'

There is a silence before Sarah says, 'Thank you.'

'Go. I have candlesticks to clean.'

BEYOND LOVE

I SIT IN MY BLACK LEATHER Eames chair at night, with my legs on the footstool, and smoke a few joints. My building is on the bank of the Thames, and it looks like a great ocean liner. I look out of the floor-to-ceiling windows at cranes that rise from the ground like giant one-eyed insects, their red eyes a warning to the helicopters that fly day and night to the nearby heliport. There are always cranes – this city has been under construction since the Iron Age. My Madeiran maid, Immaculata, empties the roaches from my ashtray every morning, and one day she asked, 'Why does an old lady smoke drugs?'

'Why doesn't a young lady smoke drugs?' I replied.

My windows become a screen, the lights of the city disappear and the past is my present.

They said I was going on a little holiday, and they spoke as if it was a great treat. I'd never been on a holiday.

'You'll have other children to play with,' he said. 'It'll be good for you.'

'Aren't you coming with me?' I asked.

'It's a holiday for children,' he replied.

169

'The air will be very healthy. It's in the country,' said my mother.

I'd read about the country in books, so I was curious to see it.

We took a coach, and they argued all the way. They always argued, but this argument had extra heat. I became fearful about what was ahead. It was a long walk from the coach stop, and I struggled to keep up with them. They were each lost in their silent rages, oblivious to my presence. My father was carrying a suitcase, and I noticed for the first time how big it was, and realised they must have packed all my clothes.

The door to the large red-brick house was opened by a thin woman with a chin that jutted out and turned up slightly at the end, like the witches in my fairy stories. She bent down and put her warm hands around my cold face.

'Welcome, Klara. I'm sure you'll be very happy with us. Let's get you inside out of the cold. I'm Auntie Violet. I'm your house mother.'

She looked up at my parents. 'We'll take good care of her.'

My father said, 'We need to leave now to catch the next coach.'

'That's for the best.'

I turned to my parents, and in a quiet voice said, 'Don't leave me.'

My mother looked at my father, who said, 'We'll be back soon, darling.'

I looked into my mother's eyes, but she turned away. My body started trembling, and the woman who called herself my aunt put her arms tightly around me. My parents started to walk quickly away. I stood watching them until they were out of sight. They didn't look back.

Auntie Violet took me to a room where seven noisy children were eating at a long table. They ranged in age from about nine to sixteen.

She clapped her hands. 'Quiet, children. I want to introduce you to Klara.'

They all turned to stare at me. I was wearing a dark-blue wool coat with a red velvet collar that my mother had found in a second-hand shop, black patent shoes, white socks and white gloves. My hairband matched the red of my coat collar. I was small for my ten years, and slight. A boy of about thirteen started sniggering.

'I want you all to tell Klara your name.'

After they'd introduced themselves, Auntie Violet said, 'Klara, tell the other children a little about yourself – where you're from, and what your hobbies are.'

I shook my head. I had seen the hostility and scorn evoked by my appearance.

'Feeling a little shy? You'll soon get used to us.' She took my hand. 'Come and sit by me and I'll get you something to eat.'

The children shouted at each other throughout the meal, they picked up food with their hands, they spoke when their mouths were full and they elbowed and pushed each other whenever Auntie Violet was out of the room. I couldn't touch my plate of tongue and ham and sliced white bread; I was battling to keep down a sandwich I had eaten five hours earlier.

I was left alone with the other children in the games room after the meal. They crowded around me, and a tall, ungainly girl of about fifteen who had food stains on her jumper asked, 'Where you from?'

I didn't answer.

'If you don't answer I'll slap you.'

I remained silent. The girl raised her hand and hit me hard on the side of the head. I was knocked off balance and had to grab the back of a chair to stop myself falling. I started to cry very quietly.

'Leave her alone, you little bitch.' It was the voice of the oldest boy in the group. He moved so that he was standing between me and the girl. He pushed his face up against hers; she turned, gave my ankle a hard kick and walked out of the room. The group dispersed to play games. I found a copy of *Alice's Adventures in Wonderland* on a bookshelf and took it to a corner, where I pretended to read.

Auntie Violet came to tell us it was bedtime at nine o'clock. She took me by the hand, saying, 'I'll show you to your room, Klara. You'll be sharing with Julie. I've unpacked your clothes and hung them up, because I know you must be very tired.'

We climbed a wide set of stairs covered in green linoleum, and walked along a dark corridor that smelled of disinfectant. She opened the last door and I saw the girl who had hit me sitting on one of the two beds in the room. She stared hard at me, and the message was clear: she'd make my life hell if I reported what she had done.

'Julie will show you where the bathroom is, and there's a towel on your bed. Sleep well, children, and I'll see you in the morning.' She closed the door quietly behind her.

I stood by the entrance, unable to move.

'You can't stand there all night. If you do what I tell you to do, you'll be all right. You make my bed in the mornings, and do the washing up when I'm on the rota. You understand?'

I nodded. I saw my pyjamas laid out on the bed next to a towel, and it was comforting to see something familiar. I moved over to the bed and undressed quickly, aware that I was being watched. I got into bed and pulled the heavy white counterpane over my head. I shut my eyes and I was adrift on a vast, dark ocean with no glimmer of light.

My parents were Polish, and they had brought me up to have the manners and graciousness of the Warsaw upper-middle class to which they belonged. We lived in one room in London, but the room was in Hampstead, so I went to school with the daughters of successful professional men, and I spoke like my classmates. The children in the home quickly learned to copy my accent and mimic my gestures and walk. I became the main source of entertainment in the house. Auntie Violet loved my good manners and general obedience, but the more she favoured me, the more the other children disliked me.

I walked to the front gate every evening at the time my parents had brought me to the house, and I waited for them. I was standing at the gate in the rain one evening when Julie came up to me and said, 'They're never coming back. No one leaves here, except to go to prison, but you're too young for that.'

I slowly lifted my hand and hit her very hard across the face. She ran inside and came back with Auntie Violet.

'Klara, I'm so disappointed in you. How could you let me down like this?'

It was a year before they came back for me. I found out a long time later that they had gone back to Poland to see if they could have a better life there, but it was too late – there was no one left who could help them. My father was the son of a rich factory owner, and he had been brought up to work in the family business. My mother was the daughter of a successful lawyer, and her upbringing had prepared her to manage a house full of servants.

They came back to London and my father eventually got a job as maître d' in a Polish club, where his class and style were put to good use. He trained the waiters and made sure the table linen, cutlery and glassware created the ambience of an aristocratic Polish home. He could finally afford to rent a flat with two rooms.

I felt nothing for my parents when I went back to live with them. And they were too busy living out the tragedy of their unhappy marriage to notice. They should have separated, but their mutual dislike and disappointment was more binding than love.

Immaculata brings me breakfast in bed every morning. I call her Immaculata because she's the best cleaner I've ever had. She buys pain au chocolat at the French bakery, and heats them until the chocolate starts to melt. If the chocolate has melted too much, she has to go back to the bakery to buy more. I read the newspapers on my laptop after breakfast and see how my investments are doing, and I chat to friends on the phone until my masseur arrives at midday.

I did a secretarial course when I was sixteen, so that I could escape the battlefield of my parents' marriage. I was hungry for life, and life was to be found in the music business in 1960s London, so I got a job as a typist for a record company. I made friends with the talent scouts, and I went with them to bars and nightclubs to hear the bands they were interested in signing. I met good-looking young men who believed I could influence their careers, and I slept with most of them. I had a fragile beauty that men found very attractive, because it made them feel protective towards me.

I shared a flat in Earl's Court with three other girls, who also worked as secretaries. One of them was called Georgina, and she worked for an auction house that sold valuable paintings. We'd cleared up after a party at the flat one night and were having a drink before going to bed when she asked, 'Why don't you ever get upset when you break up with someone? And why do you never get jealous or possessive?'

I put down my glass of wine and looked at her. 'I don't get upset for the same reason that I don't feign interest when men talk endlessly about themselves. And it's the reason I don't cook for them or put up with bad sex.'

'Are you implying I do those things?'

'You and your friends treat men as if they're minor deities.'

'That's ridiculous. Fred treats me very well.'

'I've seen how bored you look when he talks about his job. And I've no doubt you have the same expression when you're having sex.'

'You know nothing about our sex life.'

'Women are noisy when they're having good sex.'

She blushed.

'Are you some kind of feminist?'

175

'I don't know what I am, but I do know that giving away your power never ends well.'

I hadn't given an honest answer to her question because I had no idea why I didn't spend nights crying into my pillow over boyfriends. And I had no interest in finding out why I was different. I came to regret the conversation with Georgina on the many nights when I was woken by the unmistakable sounds of a woman having an orgasm.

Immaculata prepares me a lunch of fresh fish – usually scallops or halibut – and salad. And I have a glass of good white burgundy. I never let myself get fat for fear of losing the appeal of my fragility. I play poker on the internet in the afternoon. I don't play for high stakes – at least, they're not high for me, but I like to think my opponents bleed a little when I win.

I was twenty-six when I went to work in the city for a company that insured cargo ships. The only man in our department who didn't flirt with me was called Ben. There was a photo of his wife and two daughters on his desk, and he never came for drinks after work. He was very tall, and slightly stooped, as if he was trying to shorten himself. He looked older than his forty years because he was greying at the sides. There was something in his face that made you feel good when you looked at him – maybe it was kindness.

No one believes that I didn't know about his background when I decided I wanted him. I don't think even Ben believed it. His maternal grandfather had owned a company that built ocean liners, and his mother left Ben a fortune when she died. He worked because he had seen what happens to rich men who don't work.

When his PA went on maternity leave, I took over her job. He wasn't the kind of man who could be seduced by low-cut blouses or tight skirts, so one evening, after we'd worked late to meet a deadline, I told him about my time in the children's home. He talked about how he was bullied in his public school, and he revealed things to me that he had never told anyone.

He left his wife when I told him I was pregnant with his son. He didn't want to leave her, but he was too good a man to abandon me. When our son Jack was born, I knew I didn't have it in me to be a good mother, so I hired a lonely young Italian girl called Anya, who was in need of someone to love. She came to live with us, and she devoted her life to Jack. She didn't leave until the day he left for university. He grew up bilingual, because Anya spoke Italian to him, and he now works as a lawyer in Rome. He married an Italian girl, and Anya has moved in with them to look after their children. Giving him to Anya was the most loving act of my life.

Ben died a long time ago. His ex-wife blamed me for his early death. She claimed I made his life hell whenever he was in contact with her or his daughters. I can't see how a little shouting and door slamming could kill a man.

The scene I love to see play out across my dark windows is the day I called on my father and told him I was taking him on a holiday. My mother had recently died, and he wasn't coping well without her.

'Where are we going?' he asked, as I helped him into my Porsche.

'To the country. It's a surprise.'

He talked about the past during the journey – the happy years before I was born.

After three hours, we drove up a private road until we reached a huge grey stone building with turrets at each end and a rampart between them.

'Funny-looking hotel,' he said. 'You'd think they'd do more with the garden.'

I left him in the car while I went to the reception with his suitcase. When I'd signed all the paperwork, I came out for him, accompanied by two staff members dressed in blue plastic coats.

'You took your time,' he said. 'Who are these women? They're not very glamorous.'

'Put your arm over my shoulder while I help you out of the car.'

'I don't like this place.'

'Come on, Papa. I have an appointment back in London. I need to leave now.'

'I thought you were coming with me.'

'No.'

I watched him in my car mirror as I drove slowly down the long drive. The two nurses were struggling to hold him back.

FALLING TOGETHER

H E'S LEAVING ME. I stare at the blue screen on my office desk, and see his treacherous face. He lay next to me for months, planning. He made love to me. I hear a baby crying in the waiting room, and I too want to wail.

She'll be older and bruised, like I was. He'll be kind and warm. He'll cook for her. She'll feel she has come home at last. He'll be a good lover.

'We never said for ever.'

We never said 'only for as long as it suits you'.

He was writing his novel – a novel about a hero who was rescued from a turbulent life by a quiet love. We worked on a plan for a basement extension. We bought tickets for a trip to Ethiopia. I thought we'd grow old by a wild sea.

Other people are characters he edits out of the next draft of his life. I'm scared. I'm scared of going home tonight to an unlit, empty house.

The waiting room is full of angry and frightened people, but only the babies can cry. I press keys to display the name of my first patient on a screen. She has top billing in a show no one wants to be part of, including me. The others will stare at her, hoping she won't have many ailments.

Miss Spence is seventy-five years old; her grey hair is set in neat curls, and she's wearing a plum-coloured suit with a carefully ironed cream blouse. She is small and slight and there is sweetness in her pale face. Her loneliness fills the room.

'I feel tired all the time, Doctor. I find myself going to bed earlier and earlier. It's not like me. Maybe I'm anaemic.'

I look at her file on the computer and ask, 'Do you mind if I call you Lily?'

'Please do, Doctor.'

'Tell me about your life, Lily. What work did you do? Do you live with family?'

She starts to weep.

'I'm so sorry. I don't want to take up too much of your time.'

I turn my chair away from the computer. 'We'll take as much time as we need.'

Gratitude lights her face. 'It was difficult for him; his wife had been an invalid for many years, and they had a son. I was his secretary, and we fell in love. We weren't bad people – there was nothing else we could do. We were together for thirty years, but he continued to live with his wife. Nobody knew about us. He was my life, and when he died, my life ended.'

'I'm so sorry, Lily.'

'I don't regret loving him – it was my great joy, but it's hard to… carry on without him.'

'Do you live alone, Lily?'

'He bought a flat for me – it's in a big block, but most of the other flats are rented out, and the tenants don't stay long.'

'Lily, would you think of living with people your own age?'

She looks flustered. 'The flat is all I have left of him. We bought the furniture together, he put up the shelves, he hung the pictures... sometimes I feel... his presence. Is that strange, Doctor?'

'No, Lily. Grief finds consolation where it can.'

'It would be like leaving him. I couldn't do it when he was alive, and it wouldn't be any easier now he's dead.'

'What about friends? Do you see friends?'

'I couldn't get close to anyone at work in case they discovered our secret. And I wasn't from London, so I didn't have childhood friends here.'

Her lover was a vampire who gorged on her life, but she sees herself as the heroine in a tragic love story; it is the only narrative she can live with.

'I understand, Lily.'

'His son takes me out to lunch when he comes to London – he sees me as an old family friend – but he looks so like his father when he was young, I feel upset for days afterwards.'

There is nothing I can say.

'I mustn't take up any more of your time. There are sick people who need to see you, Doctor.'

'Lily, make another appointment so we can talk again.'

'Thank you, Doctor.'

She won't come back. She will not give up the companionship of her ghost.

He's packing his clothes; his shirts will be neatly folded. He'll have plastic crates for his books. He'll take the paintings I gave him as presents because I loved them, and I loved him. They will hang on her walls. I turned him into my wife.

A young woman in jeans and T-shirt with a child in a pram enters the room. She looks exhausted, and her hair is unwashed. Her T-shirt has an image of an explosion on the front – it looks as if her breasts have been blown up.

'He has a bug of some kind, and he isn't getting better. I'm afraid it might develop into something worse.'

She avoids eye contact.

'Let's have a look at him.'

I examine the child and see that he has a cold. He is otherwise healthy and well cared for. He laughs when I smile at him. His clothes and pram are expensive – she is not on benefits.

'Nothing to worry about,' I say. 'He's doing very well. You're a good mum.'

She doesn't react. Her eyes are dead. She's not here; she's not in the room.

'How are you doing? It's not an easy time, is it?'

'I'm fine.'

Her tone is flat. She's as far from fine as I am.

'Are you getting enough sleep?'

'I catch up when he has his nap in the afternoon.'

'Is your partner able to give much support?'

'He's back at work.'

'Are you going to any mother-and-baby groups?'

'They're not my kind of gig.'

They wouldn't have been mine either.

'Do you have family and friends living near you?'

She suddenly looks very angry and says, 'I shouldn't have come here.'

She stands up, and starts to leave the room.

'Katherine, I want to help. Tell me what I can do.'

She doesn't answer. She pulls the hood up on the pram and hurries from the room without looking back.

I feel uneasy about her. I spend time deciding what to put in her notes.

Sheila, one of the older secretaries, comes into my office with a cup of strong tea. The fat from thousands of biscuits lies on her hips, and she limps because she won't have surgery on her arthritic knee. We have worked together for many years, and she's noticed that I'm behaving like a second-rate actress struggling with the role of a doctor. She knows better than to ask any questions. I look away from the kindness in her eyes.

It'll take him less than a day to remove his presence. I will lie awake all night haunted by his absence.

The splash of yellow in Mr Hemmings' tie suggests he is more interesting than his navy business suit would imply. He is a slim fifty-year-old who recently had two stents inserted. He seems reluctant to sit down, as if he might have to make a quick getaway.

'The operation went well,' I say.

'Yes, the surgeon was very pleased.'

'And you're back at work?'

'Yes.'

There was a silence.

'You're wondering why I made the appointment?'

'Are you having side effects from the medication?'

'I'm having side effects from nearly dying.'

'It's a lot to come to terms with.'

He leans forward, and there's urgency in his eyes. 'I never thought about my life before the heart attack, but since I left hospital I feel as if it's someone else's life, and I don't think it's the life I want. I worked long hours and didn't see much of my family. Work was like a sport to me, and I loved winning. I'd been a talented athlete when I was young. And now I leave hundreds of emails unopened every day and sit at meetings where I feel that nothing we talk about matters. I lie next to my wife at night, and she feels like a stranger. I don't think we've been close for years. I watch my children, and I'm not sure I like them. That's a terrible thing to say, I know.'

He waits for me to respond, but I don't say anything.

'I sometimes wonder if it's because my arteries were blocked that I don't care about the people, the things I cared about. My heart wasn't getting enough blood for a long time.'

'Mr Hemmings, this isn't a medical problem.'

'I know it isn't, but it would be so much easier if it was.'

'And I don't think you need to see a psychologist.'

'It's an existential problem, but who do I go to with that?'

'If there was a profession that could tell us how to live our lives, the waiting lists would be very long.'

He laughs. 'Part of me wants to become the person I was again, and another part of me despises him.'

'Time is the great problem solver.'

'I nearly ran out of that.'

'The stents have replenished your stock.'

'I am very grateful, and that's why I want to use it well – but I don't know what it means to live a good life. I don't know how to live any more.' He sighs and looks around the room. 'I know you can't do anything. I came here because I needed to hear myself say those things. I feel… clearer now. Thank you.'

'It's not easy for anyone.'

'People don't let on.'

'No.'

'I suppose things might fall apart if they did.'

'Or fall together.'

'I think I need to fall together.'

He stands and puts out his hand. I take it, and it's good to feel the touch of another human. We smile at each other, and he leaves the room.

I bump into a colleague in the corridor. 'Lunch?' she asks.

'Sorry. I'm going for a run.'

She married a man who will never leave her. Her children won't take drugs or need abortions. She will never wake in the night worrying about a young woman with a baby.

'Come for dinner soon. I'll text some dates.'

I'd rather be waterboarded.

I drive to a park a few miles away. I'll walk, because it will give me more time – time to cry for my loss and the losses of the world.

THE VULNERABLE HOUR

I T WAS THIRTY MINUTES before the vulnerable hour, but the supermarket car park was almost full. A long, undulating tail of pensioners stretched out behind the closed glass doors. Gloved hands held tightly on to trolleys, and there was fear in the eyes that stared at the back of the person ahead. Few spoke.

The doors didn't open for five long minutes after eight, five precious minutes of the sixty allocated to them. A member of staff stood at each side of a partially opened door, deciding who could enter. A man in his thirties was shouting and swearing at them. Courtney Taylor guarded the left side of the entrance. His grandmother had been sent back to Barbados a year earlier because she didn't have the papers to prove she'd come to England as a child. She had taken him in when he ran away from home to escape his stepfather. Negus Tasifa stood at the right side of the entrance. He was a refugee from Ethiopia who had spent a year in a detention centre before being allowed live in the country. A scar stretched along the side of his head, as if his head had been cracked open with a spoon.

Jack Watson was leaning against the wall of the super-market, smoking a cigarette and watching the crowd push-ing against each other. His copies of *The Big Issue* were at his feet; he knew the customers wouldn't buy from him until they were on their way out. The wife he had found on the internet had come over from the Philippines to live with him in his one-room flat a few weeks earlier. He told her he worked for a newspaper.

Elizabeth Devereux was stretching out a hand covered in a burgundy leather glove to take the last fresh chicken from a refrigerated cabinet when a hand in a blue kitchen glove shot out from the other side and grabbed it. She turned to the woman who had stolen her prize and shouted, 'You bitch! I've had cancer.'

Maggie Kane was wearing a cotton coat that was too big for her, and her grey hair needed cutting. She started to cry. 'My grandson lives with me; his mother died, and he needs the protein.' Her daughter was in prison, but the consequences were the same for the boy.

'Oh, God, I'm so sorry!' Elizabeth covered her mouth with her hand.

'Don't touch your mouth.'

'Thank you. I'm so sorry I shouted at you. I don't know what's happening to me. It's—'

'I know. We're not ourselves.'

'Keep the chicken – you need it more than I do.'

'No,' said Maggie. 'You should be eating well to stop the cancer coming back.' She held the chicken out in both hands.

'A child needs good nutrition. I can't take it.'

'Maybe we could cut it in two?'

Elizabeth smiled. 'The till wouldn't be able to cope with that!'

'We have a world full of computers, but they can do nothing for us now. I could give you pasta – it was on the special-offers shelf because its packaging is a bit battered.'

'Oh, I'd love some pasta; I haven't been able to get any for three weeks. I've frozen pasta sauces, but I haven't had anything to eat with them.'

Maggie gave her two large bags of penne.

'Thank you so much.'

'I'll make soup and it'll last us for weeks; he loves it.'

'I'm glad.'

'God bless you.'

'Thank you.'

Maggie admired Elizabeth's white wool coat as she walked away; only the rich could afford the dry-cleaning bills for a white coat.

Customers were moving quickly up and down the aisles, grabbing what they needed before the shelves emptied. Sally Martin was staring at a tall man wearing a cobalt-blue cashmere jumper who was coming towards her. He was sauntering as if he was walking along a seaside promenade. 'That's the kind of man I should have married,' she thought. She smiled at him as if to say, 'We're better than them,' and he smiled back. His teeth were as white as the surgical mask worn by the woman walking behind him, and Sally closed her mouth to conceal the teeth she wasn't quite vain enough to whiten. She looked in his basket – wine, goat's cheese, smoked salmon. No toilet rolls or hand sanitiser. He was doing his normal shop – he wasn't going to push people out of his way or jump the long queues at the till. He was civilised. She felt a little sad after he'd passed her, and tried not to dwell on all the disastrous choices she had made.

Ben Drysdale was remembering the men he had picked up in this supermarket after the clubs closed. It was open all night in those days, and gay men came here to buy booze to take to parties. His diagnosis didn't change anything – he limited himself to other men who had the virus. He had to admit, he derived a certain pleasure from seeing the rest of the world experience the terror that once had infected him. He no longer feared death; he had lived three decades longer than expected, and he had made his peace with it. Sex had been his life's obsession. He worked in a job he disliked to earn enough to afford the lifestyle that would make him attractive to other men. His friends shared his obsession; they hunted in packs. His body had provided warm hospitality to every sexually transmitted disease that came to the city. It would be ironic if what he called the 'straight virus' saw him off.

He wondered sometimes if he should have married and had sex as a hobby. Women had always been attracted to him. That elegant woman with the warm smile he had just passed might have been a good companion. But a wife would have wanted children, and he couldn't stand the noise and mess and smells that came with children; they offended him aesthetically. He headed towards the health aisle to buy condoms.

Lucy Nelson had never been to this supermarket before, but she'd researched the layout online. She was wearing a white surgical mask, disposable gloves and clothes she only wore outdoors. She was in her fifties, but she'd got into the supermarket during the vulnerable hour because she'd shown her dead mother's birth certificate to Negus Tasifa, and told him she was her mother's carer. She'd left her younger girlfriend, Clare, at home, because Clare would have refused to wear a mask and would have chatted to everyone. They'd had an argument that morning. After they'd listened to the first news bulletin, Clare said, 'I'm going to volunteer to work at a hospital.'

'It's out of the question,' she had replied. 'You'd be exposed to the virus numerous times a day, and the patients who die are the ones exposed to it most often.'

'I have to do something!'

'Doing nothing *is* doing something – it's stopping the transmission.'

'It's not enough.'

'Well, dying isn't going to help anyone.'

'I don't want to come out of it knowing all I did was save my own skin.'

'I trust you not to put me at risk – it's not just about you!'

'The NHS will save our lives if we get it; I want to help them.'

'But you don't have the skills they need.'

'They need drivers to bring medicine from pharmacies to the hospital, and to drive patients to the hospital and back home.'

'You're a terrible driver!'

'Well, there's no traffic. If the NHS doesn't need me, I could deliver food to old people who are isolated.'

'You hated visiting my mother.'

'She was poisonous.'

'You just have a fantasy about being a hero from all those children's books you loved.'

'You don't believe in altruism?'

'I think altruism fulfils the needs of the giver as much as the recipient.'

'I hate cynicism.'

'It's not cynicism – it's an acknowledgement of the complexity of human motivation and...'

They had argued until it was time for Lucy to leave. And now she was going over and over the things they'd said to each other when her mind should have been fully concentrated on getting the food they needed. A man leaning on a stick was moving slowly down the aisle, blocking her way. When he reached the woman next to her, he took his hand from behind his back and held up a four-pack of tinned tomatoes. His wife screamed with joy, threw her arms around him and kissed him. Lucy said a prayer to a god she had long ago stopped believing in that she and Clare would not split up.

Elizabeth Devereux didn't realise until it was too late to move away that the person in the queue ahead of her was the woman who took the chicken. Elizabeth was still feeling ashamed of having shouted at her.

'The tills have crashed', said Maggie. She was admiring Elizabeth's carefully applied make-up; she was the kind of woman who would be putting clean sheets on the bed while bombs were dropping.

'The gods really have it in for us,' said Elizabeth.

'Did you get everything you needed?'

'Most things – it's much better than last week!'

'Last week was frightening.'

'It really was.'

They were silent for a while. A member of staff apologised over a public-address system for the delay, and reassured them that engineers would soon have the tills working again.

'It must have been awful to lose a child,' said Elizabeth.

'She's in prison. I didn't want you to think we were that kind of family.'

'I'm sorry.' She knew she'd have lied in the same situation.

'She got in with the wrong crowd at school and left without any qualifications, and it's hard to get by on the minimum wage. I should have been stricter with her when she was young, but I didn't want my child to be frightened of me.'

'I discovered our daughter was smoking marijuana when she was thirteen, so I sent her to boarding school. She did well and went to university, but we haven't been close since I sent her away.' Elizabeth had never told anyone she wasn't close to Gillian. Her friends knew all about Gillian's job at an investment bank in New York, but they didn't know the one thing that really mattered. 'She phones regularly, but it's out of duty, not love.'

'That's hard.'

Maggie looked directly into Elizabeth's eyes, and Elizabeth knew the other woman had experienced the desolation that only love can bring.

'My daughter tried to smuggle a suitcase of cocaine into Heathrow,' said Maggie. 'She wanted to buy a flat for herself and her son – she was tired of having to move every time the rent was raised. It was wrong, and stupid.'

'None of us know what we'd do if we were desperate.'

'I suppose you're right.'

'Is your husband living with you?'

'He died when my daughter was eight. He worked with asbestos.' Her face lit up from within when she remembered him, and Elizabeth got a glimpse of the lovely young woman she must once have been.

'How sad.'

'I thought I was coping, but looking back, I was doolally. And that must have affected my daughter.'

'It wasn't your fault.'

'No.'

They were silent again.

'It's not easy being alone at a time like this, is it?' asked Elizabeth.

'Being in an unhappy relationship would be worse – I hear my neighbours.'

'I often long for neighbours I could hear; most of the flats in my building are owned by people who live in Moscow. I live in Chelski,' she said, with a smile.

'Is your husband alive?'

'He too succumbed to an occupational hazard – an office full of young women.'

Maggie laughed.

'I divorced him a long time ago.'

Maggie noticed the man in front of her had moved forward. 'Ah, the tills are working again.'

'Great.' Elizabeth looked into her trolley. 'I'm so glad I've got the pasta.'

When it was Maggie's turn to put her food on the conveyer belt, she turned to Elizabeth and said, 'It's been good talking to you.'

'And you!'

'There's only so much you can talk about with a ten-year-old boy.'

'There's only so much you can talk about with yourself! I hope your daughter comes home soon.'

'Thank you.'

Elizabeth watched Maggie limp away, carrying two heavy bags of shopping, and she thought about how nice it would be to have her as a neighbour.

A SPLASH OF WORDS

THE LIGHT CREEPS UNDER the shutters, seeking living things. I hide beneath the eiderdown. Eiderdown: I like the old words. I imagine a black-and-white drake and his brown mate riding the swell of the Irish Sea.

Maybe I won't get up today. I did try not getting up once. The phone rang unanswered, like a bird seeking a mate. A shoal of letters lay on the hall floor. Callers walked slowly away from the unyielding door. They thought I'd left town. After ten days I felt like a whiskey, so I got up. I resurrected myself. The sunlight was too bright, the cars too loud.

I live in the Artist's studio. The Artist is long dead, but his studio lives on. He liked to dismember me on canvas. The paintings sold. We partied.

I am disfigured now by the artist age. The Artist now works on my flesh and in my bones. He deforms my hands and slashes at my hip.

The past is my present, and soon it will be my future.

I have imaginary lovers – collages of those I have loved. They have the Artist's broad back, the Spaniard's mouth, the Poet's laugh and the Dutchman's cold eyes.

The Artist knocked down the dividing walls, so I can see the kitchen sink and the old pine table from my bed, and on the other side I see the claw-foot bath he found in a skip. The floorboards are covered with splashes of the colours he loved – blues, whites and greys.

I lived once before in a room without walls.

> Hail Mary, full of Grace,
> The Lord is with thee;
> Blessed art thou among women...

We were woken every morning in our white-curtained cubicles by a joyless rendering of the prayer. It was the voice of a woman who had married God in the hope of finding love. It was the voice of a disappointed woman. We washed in white porcelain basins while we answered the rosary. We walked in a silent line to the chapel for Mass. We thought we were privileged.

Today I am called to life by the muezzin light. I leave the large bed and limp to the table to grind coffee beans. I use an old macchinetta to make the coffee – I love its pleated skirt and elegantly cocked handle. I heat milk. I move the shutters a little – there is gold in the morning light; it is a day to celebrate. I put on a Brandenburg concerto and listen to the flute and strings chase each other around the room.

I treat myself to Louis MacNeice; I recite 'Entirely' over and over, like a prayer.

I am ready to go all the way – to fully open the shutters. When my eyes recover from the assault of the light, I look down at the cars: they never waver when they stop at the lights. They don't find themselves wandering back to where they've been.

I run the bath and gather my towels. When I slowly lower myself into the warm water, I feel my body lighten and my limbs move freely again. My body rewards me with feelings of deep pleasure for giving it a reprieve from gravity. There is a painting of me in this bath – it hangs on a stranger's wall.

I dry myself by gently patting my limbs with the towel – the way the Artist used to dry me. Not the harsh sawing movements my mother used to dry my small body. I put on a blue silk kimono and start applying my make-up. I still have my admirers; I don't disappoint them. Time, who has taken so much, has spared me my cheekbones and my turf-brown eyes. My admirers gaze through the clouds of their cataracts and see the woman I once was.

It is a day for reds and greens, scarves and noisy jewellery. The Artist made jewellery for me – boisterous, flashing necklaces, clamouring earrings.

I make my way slowly down the four flights of stairs. 'Flight' – I did a lot of flighting. Wood is showing through the aged linoleum at the centre of the steps. I lean on my stick for a rest on each landing. The Artist and I used to run up these flights, eager to make love.

The artist age is slashing at my hip again – he is working with élan today. They tell me I need a new hip. The greedy children of the Artist will sell the studio if I leave. They want money. We all want. I wanted love. I am Keeper of the Artist's shrine.

I was barren, so my life was fertile.

'Isn't it time you settled down?' she'd ask time and again in her letters. I wanted none of her settling. I had seen what was in the eyes of the settled.

She made up stories. I was a teacher, a social worker. I was engaged. I had been jilted. I was anything other than what I was. I like to think that if I had a child, I would let them be.

I have made it to the street. It is ten minutes to my destination. I have tried to count the steps, but my mind skedaddles off. It was always a skedaddling mind.

I met the Dutchman at a party. He stood alone, taller than everyone else, at the back of the room, hands behind his back. He was a general in search of an enemy. He looked at me, and I found myself moving towards him. When I reached him, he said, 'Come with me. We go to your place.'

He made love as if he'd hated me all his life. I thought he was going to kill me. When I woke in the morning, he was gone. All that was left was the smell of his Gitanes and my pillaged body.

A few weeks later, I arrived home to find him in my flat: he had broken in.

'I stay for a few weeks.'

He must have been in hiding, because he never left the flat. And he wouldn't let me answer the phone or doorbell. He played Mahler all day, and he cooked, because he said my cooking was an insult. He wouldn't let me work. And at night he took me to the wild, desolate shores of an island far beyond the land of love.

One evening I came home with the sweetbreads he'd asked me to buy that afternoon, and he had gone. A week later, I phoned the host of the party where I'd met him, and asked if he knew anything about him.

'Well', he said, 'there are many stories, so take your pick. Some say he's a spy, and if he is, he's sure to be a double agent. Others say he imports heroin from Afghanistan. Someone swore blind he sells arms to repressive regimes. There's also a story about him being a great pianist who had his fingers broken when he was a prisoner of war. He is, I suppose, what you want him to be.'

He would reappear every few months, and would never talk about where he'd been or when he would leave. I became someone who waited, someone who was never where they were.

Once when he returned in the middle of the night, I said, 'I might not have been alone.'

He sat on a kitchen chair in his long black leather coat, and took off his boots before he answered. 'There will never be anyone here. You are alive with me. You are alive with me because you are close to death. We need to be close to death to feel truly alive.'

He took off his coat and went into the bedroom. He lay on the bed in his clothes and slept for two days. I sat and watched him – watched his bristles grow and listened to his breathing. I was alone in an indifferent universe, and he was my saviour.

When he woke the morning of the third day, he went to the kitchen and took a bottle of brandy from his coat pocket. We drank the brandy and made love all that day. On the following day he left again.

I had friends, a couple, who understood how dangerous he was. So they came to my flat one evening, and started packing my belongings.

'What are you doing?' I asked.

'We're taking you to our house in France. You have to escape this man – he will destroy you. If you leave the flat, he won't be able to find you.'

I lived in their house in Collias for a year. I was a woman in a cubist painting, and I had to reassemble the fragments of myself. I never saw the Dutchman again.

I was an artist's model – I was the one they all wanted to paint. I never let myself be seduced by them because I had to let them inside me, to feel me, to be me, and sex would have kept them out. I didn't let the Artist paint me until we had been lovers for many years.

The Poet was a small man with big ambitions. I met him at the opening of an exhibition. He came up to me and said, 'You are the most beautiful woman here, and I am a poet, so you should come home with me.'

I laughed.

'I don't give up – on poetry or on women. Some day you will be mine.'

He found out where I lived and he started drinking in my local pub. He got to know my friends.

One night I came home from a party to find him sitting on the step outside my flat.

'I could immortalise you,' he said. 'You could be my Maud Gonne.'

'Maud Gonne didn't need Yeats to immortalise her.'

'Maybe not, but you need me.'

'Why?'

'Because you have no country to free, and no children. None of us want to be forgotten.'

'We'll all be forgotten.'

'Yeats isn't.'

'Being immortalised only matters if you believe in immortality. Goodnight,' I said, and put my key in the lock of the front door.

'But I need you – I need you!' he shouted.

'Love has nothing to do with need. Take your need somewhere else,' I said, and went into the house.

He was back the next night, and all the following nights, until I gave in. His noise filled an emptiness within me.

He would observe me for hours with the intensity of a painter, and then he'd write his poems. The poems didn't seem to have anything to do with me, but he said they were all about me. He wrote of the cranes that stretch their long metal necks above city buildings, like prehistoric reptiles. He wrote of the screams of urban vixens piercing the silence of the night. And he wrote of the old men who sit alone in parks, waiting for death.

He was ruthless with his words – he crossed them out with savagery, he shoved and pushed them around his poems. He went to parties, searching for people who would make him famous. He always had an appetite for love, but the table manners of a stray dog. Schoolchildren now study the poems he wrote on my body.

He had abandoned a wife and children. His children would sometimes visit us. He would look for himself in them, and favour those who were like him. When he became a great man, he was always photographed with the family he had abandoned.

I don't remember why we parted. Perhaps he found success a better companion than me.

I turn a corner and see the next corner after which my destination will be in sight. The pain has developed a rhythm; it quickens with each step. I have gone too far to turn back.

I met the Spaniard on a street in Barcelona. I was walking back to my hotel with a friend on a hot summer night. We came upon a group of men dancing flamenco in a square. We stood, unable to take our eyes from them until they stopped, many hours later. He came over to me, put his arm lightly around my waist and started to waltz around the square with me. Another of the dancers waltzed with my friend. They drove us to the beach to see the sunrise. We stood silent on the sand, watching the sun, like Pagans paying homage to their god. And afterwards we let fresh croissants melt on our tongues, as if they had been consecrated.

He was a dancer who lived the dance. We went to live in a fisherman's cottage in Cadaqués. He knew all the artists who went there to paint. We would sleep until late in the afternoon, when we'd swim off the rocks. In the evenings, we ate fish, drank wine and danced with our friends until the sky lightened. In time, I grew weary of the dance. He raised his head in the air, clicked his fingers and danced all the way back to his wife when he found me with the Artist.

I will be buried next to the Artist's gnawed bones. He will turn his empty eye sockets to me and say, 'What took you so long?' – as he used to when he raced me up the stairs. He will take me in his arms, and I will never wake alone again.

I have arrived. I open the pub door and stand at the entrance while the landlady stretches out her arms and says, 'She's here at last! We've been waiting for you – it's Jack's birthday, so it's drinks on the house.'

'Very kind,' I say, and try not to limp on the way to our table in the corner.

Jack gets up slowly to embrace me. He was the Artist's friend, and he likes to think he takes care of me for his friend. Jack was also a painter, but he destroyed everything he painted because they never matched the masterpieces in his head. He was the only real artist. He wears young men's clothes – a grey hooded sweatshirt and jeans. He pays young men to make love to him, in the hope that one of them will be the great love he has been seeking for so long. The Captain is next to embrace me. I like the brush of his well-tended moustache against my face. The stripes of his suit are unfashionably wide, and I know he has carefully ironed each pleat of his white shirt.

'The most beautiful woman in London,' he says, as he struggles back to his seat.

'My darling, you'll forgive me if I don't get up to greet you,' said Johnny, who is sitting between the other two, a crutch by his chair.

Johnny's large round head is always bent forward slightly, as if he's about to headbutt the person next to him. He continues with a story he has been telling. 'I opened the door of the bedroom, thinking it was Daphne's. The room was completely dark, so I felt my way along the wall until I reached the bed. I assumed she must be asleep, so I thought I'd wake her with a pleasant surprise,' he said, laughing like a schoolboy. 'I slipped in beside her and put my hand under her nightdress. My hand had just started on its journey north when the eighty-year-old dowager switched on the bedside lamp and said, "Johnny

Davenport, I could have you arrested for this, and I will if you don't continue!"'

We laugh for a long time, as we always do. We tell each other the same stories, again and again. They are the polished pebbles washed up by our lives. We have no new stories.

The landlady, Carmel, comes over with a tray of drinks. She is a big woman with wild black hair. Her parents came from Connemara. She puts the glass of Laphroaig in front of me with a wink, and I realise she has poured me a double. If the Captain and Johnny order lunch later, she will bring food for Jack and me and not charge us for it. She does this often – it is the only hot food we eat.

The Captain is telling one of his stories. I swirl the hay-yellow drink in the glass. I add a little water; I take a sip, and taste burning turf. The drink from Islay tastes of Ireland. I take another sip, stare into the glass and see myself on top of a cart-load of turf. We are returning from the bog on a summer afternoon. I am thrown about in the turf as the old donkey stumbles on the dirt road. My uncle and cousin are laughing at the sight of five-year-old me in my city dress, being tossed around on a sea of turf.

'It'll burn well, that one,' says my cousin, Paky.

'It will surely,' says my uncle, laughing.

I have been running free over the bog all day, like a tinker child, while my uncle and cousin cut and turn the turf. We have drunk sweet tea from a whiskey bottle and eaten my aunt's fresh bread with raspberry jam made from berries that grow wild in the woods behind the cottage. The heat of the sun is smouldering under my skin. I am happy and scared, scared and happy.

We have celebrated Jack's birthday, and now it's time for us to leave. Carmel comes to the door to see us off. The drinks have loosened our stiff muscles. We say our farewells – the Captain kisses my hand. Johnny gives me a tip for the 1.30 at Doncaster the following day – 'a dead cert', he says. Jack tells me about an exhibition he wants me to see, but we both know I'll never see it.

We go our separate ways. We each walk the streets where we have lived and loved, like ghosts of ourselves.

FOOTPRINTS

I WAS GOING TO MEET the old crowd. I hadn't met most of them for over thirty years. We'd shared flats, partied together and been each other's lovers. We were socialists and communists, because we believed all children had a right to flourish. We were feminists before celebrities made it fashionable, and we loved women when being a lesbian could lose you custody of your children. We were looking for new ways of being. We didn't want to own our lovers, and we weren't interested in exclusive love. But our free intellects were lumbered with primitive emotions, so there was always someone crying into their pillow.

We lived in Notting Hill Gate and Kensington in flats with high ceilings and low rents. Some of us lived in squats or social housing. I had friends who declared the streets where they squatted an independent republic: they appointed Ministers of State and had their own national newspaper and national theatre. We had separatist houses where men weren't allowed past the front door. We wrote poetry, studied sculpture and learned to play jazz. Most of us had been to university, but we had no student debt. We were free.

We lived on benefits or worked in bars and restaurants, because you didn't need much money to live. And living was what we were about.

We talked endlessly about the new world we were going to create – a world free from prejudice and free from the shadow of nuclear war. But the only political activity we engaged in was marching. We loved marching. We marched to support the miners, we marched against racism, we marched for gay rights and we marched against nuclear arms. We'd take cans of beer with us and stop off at pubs along the route for fresh supplies. We would meet everyone we knew on marches, and we'd all end up dancing the night away to a live band in a packed marquee. We were going to overcome.

When the policies of the new Conservative government kicked in, the squats disappeared, social housing was sold off and rents went up. The coal mines were closed down and whole communities were left without work. Black people were discriminated against and harassed by the police, but no one cared. Clause 28 was introduced to repress gay people. The dancing was over.

The long driveway to the crematorium is lined with yellow heleniums; I'd tried growing them but they had defeated me. I wondered if the gardener's secret was ash-rich compost. The car park is packed with people chatting and exchanging phone numbers. I stay in the car for a while, watching them. I'm pleased to see few are wearing black – Alex hated the colour.

'Emma, how nice to see you. You've hardly changed.'

The woman greeting me has short grey hair and a rust-coloured tweed jacket. I have no idea who she is.

'The last time you saw me I had green hair and wore biker leathers.'

'My God, it's you Viv,' I say. 'Have you still got the Harley?'

She laughs. 'It's in Harley heaven. I spent more time falling off that bike than I spent on it. How are you?'

She was the one who made things happen. Her eyes burned like beacons in a sea fog, but she was drawing you towards the rocks. After a night out with her, you woke the following day feeling appalled and a little thrilled by what you'd done. We'd stolen a boat on the Thames one night, and sailed for hours before abandoning it miles downriver. I hadn't recognised her because now her eyes were dead.

'I'm fine. I was very sad to hear about Alex,' I say, nodding towards the building behind us.

'Yes, it's hard to believe.'

'Were you in touch with her?'

'No. We lost contact a long time ago. And you?'

'I hadn't seen her since she moved to the country. We emailed at Christmas, but that was it.'

'I heard you became an academic,' she says.

'Yes, the real world had turned ugly, so I swam across the moat. What about you? How have you been?'

She looks like she's been living in a war zone.

'I became a full-time drinker, and that needed subsidising, so I took up card fraud, but I wasn't a very competent criminal and ended up in Holloway.'

'I'm so sorry.'

'It was the best thing that could have happened. I went into recovery and I've been sober for ten years.'

'That's fantastic.'

'And now I work as an alcohol and drug counsellor.'

'That must be rewarding.' I was thinking she needed to get away from all that darkness and get out into the sunlight.

'It is.'

'Your mother wouldn't have been thrilled about Holloway.' I'd met her mother – she was a magistrate and a scary woman.

'She was convinced I'd got myself sent to prison just to humiliate her.'

'Do you think there was something in that?'

'I've no idea. I had as much insight into why I did anything as an amoeba. She died before she got around to forgiving me.'

'I'm sorry.'

'My father visited me in prison every week.'

We have to move on to the grass to get out of the way of a white Porsche. A slim, dark-haired woman wearing a mustard coat gets out and runs towards us with her arms outstretched.

'My darlings, how wonderful to see you!' She hugs us.

Her face is familiar, but I can't place her.

'How flattering – you don't recognise me!'

She blows her cheeks out.

'Lucy!' I say.

'Bariatric surgery – I was never one for doing things the hard way.'

Lucy was the daughter of a Conservative MP; she had no interest in politics, but hung out with us because we gave the best parties.

'I've read reviews of your programmes – they're very popular,' I say.

'Of course, you're far too high-minded to watch them. Remember how contemptuous you all were when you saw me reading *The News of the World* and watching daytime TV? I knew popular culture was heading for the sewer, and I was going to be down there waiting for it. Circuses are all the public wants, and to see people in stocks, and my company provides them.'

'I have no objection to circuses, but we seem to get nothing else,' I reply.

'You overestimate the human species – it's why your socialist revolution didn't happen. All people want is a job that gives them enough money to buy junk food, and television programmes that provide material for their sexual fantasies. And as long as they believe someone is worse off than them, preferably emigrants, they're happy.'

'I'm not going to argue with you. This isn't the time—'

'I've been looking forward so much to discussing the triumph of the Right with you.'

'Everyone is going inside,' says Viv.

'I better get back to my child bride – being rich has great cachet with young Sapphists. We'll talk later.' Lucy kisses my cheek before moving away.

'What was all that about?' asks Viv.

'Ask her.' She'd once made a pass at me, and I hadn't handled the situation well.

The crematorium is packed. There are a lot of familiar faces and a cohort on one side who look like they're on their way to a hunt meeting. I stare at the oak coffin and remember the smell and taste of the body that lies under the lid. I'm glad the coffin is closed, because I want to remember her as she was the night before she left London:

her eyes wild with excitement at the prospect of starting a new life in the country.

A curtain opens on one side of the stage, and a group of middle-aged woman carrying saxophones, a trumpet and a double bass walk out. They're a group whose gigs we always went to; they're greeted with loud clapping. They start playing 'Footprints', and I'm taken back to smoky basement clubs in Peckham and Hackney, to nights when all that mattered in the world was the soulful rhythms of the music.

When they finish playing, I hear a voice saying, 'Aren't they brilliant? I want to thank you all for coming – I know you've had a journey to get here.'

We all stare in horror at the coffin, because it's Alex's voice.

'I've given you a bit of a fright, haven't I?' She laughs. 'I made this recording when I knew I was dying. Life is too short for mourning, so I want today to be a great party. I've booked a room at my club, and I want you to drink champagne and dance all night. I won't see you in the next world, because I don't believe there is one, but I'm very grateful to have known you in this world. I love you all. Live well.'

The musicians start playing 'Stairway to the Stars', and two women step in front of the stage and dance. The slow graceful movement of their bodies fills me with a longing to be in love again.

When the musicians have their next break, a tall blonde woman wearing a turquoise silk blouse and a gold chain with a pendant walks to the microphone in the centre of the stage. She looks about mid-fifties.

'I'm the widow.' She looks at her audience. 'It's OK to laugh.'

Lucy gives a wolf whistle and people laugh.

'I was a happily married woman with grown children when the force of nature that was Alex hit our village. She bought the local Georgian manor house, and we were all rather curious about her. The old couple who sold her the house told me her name, so I Googled her and learned that she had been the chief executive of a large bank, and was best known for introducing policies that improved the diversity of the staff. She had attracted a huge amount of publicity when she led by example by coming out as a lesbian. There was a lot of surprise and disappointment when she decided to resign after a few years, because the bank was doing very well. Journalists speculated that she was going to enter politics. I decided to call on her, to welcome her to the village. It was an early spring morning when I walked up the drive, and she was in the garden planting bulbs. Her jeans were torn and she was covered in mud.

'"Hello," she shouted. "You must be a native."

'I was wearing my Barbour jacket.

'"I've come to welcome you to the village," I said.

'She replied: "That's very kind of you. Let's go inside and have a glass of champagne."

'You won't be very surprised to hear that I never left…'

Listening to the widow talk about their life together, I realise it didn't matter much to Alex who she was with: she needed to always be in love, but not with the same person. And maybe that's the best way to manage the challenges of love. So many of us feel there is only person who can bring all that is good into our lives, and we spend our time regretting the one we've lost or longing for the one we can never have.

'...My only regret is that we didn't have longer together. I won't say any more, because we have a party to go to. Let's celebrate a woman who lived and loved fearlessly.'

Viv comes back to my house with me so I can drop my car off and take the dog out before going to the party. We talk about Alex while we walk in the park.

'Remember the night she walked down Kensington Church Street, hopping from car roof to car roof?' I ask.

'And when the policeman who arrested her told her she could make one phone call, she ordered a pizza.'

'I'd forgotten that,' I say, laughing. 'She wasn't charged, was she?'

'Her cousin was with the Crown Prosecution Service and he used his influence.'

I think there is resentment in Viv's voice, but I'm not sure.

'If there had been social media then, most of us would have become unemployable,' I say.

'If we'd had the internet, we'd probably never have left our flats. I'd definitely have developed a gaming addiction.'

Sadness comes off her, like mist over a pond.

The DJ at the club is playing 'Karma Chameleon', and dozens of middle-aged women and men are jumping around the dance floor. I join the queue for the buffet and find myself standing next to Bella, an old flatmate.

'I wanted children, so I married a man,' she says. 'It's so much easier – you don't have to worry about their feelings, so you can get on with your life. Women get too close.'

'Happy?' I ask.

'Yes. It's wasn't something I aspired to, so it was unexpected.'

'I think that's the best way to find it: stop looking.'

'I've had a good career, but the thing I'm proudest of is bringing up two feminist sons. If every woman brought up her sons to be feminists, we really would change the world.'

'Did other boys make fun of them when they were growing up?'

'They did – until they realised my boys were very popular with the girls, so they all started buying Caitlin Moran's books to stick out of their backpacks. I'm glad I didn't have a daughter – I'd have been terrified she'd do all the stuff we did. Remember all the hitch-hiking? And sleeping on beaches in Greece?'

I remember escaping from a car with Alex when the men who'd given us a lift started to assault us. We managed to get away because I'd used a can of hairspray to temporarily blind them – it was a tip I'd picked up in a self-defence class.

'I do remember.'

We've finished filling our plates with wild salmon and new potatoes.

'Let's keep in touch,' she says.

'Yes,' I reply, knowing we won't.

I sit next to Harriet, an old friend I still see regularly. She works as a solicitor for Legal Aid. She lived at Greenham

Common for a year, and we used to bring her emergency supplies of meat and whisky because the other women at her gate were teetotal vegetarians. Her wild hair and clothes always smelled of wood smoke.

'It's interesting to see everyone again,' I say.

'I'm glad they all came.' She's wearing a lemon silk suit that hangs beautifully, and her hair is gathered in a chignon. She's come straight from court.

'Do you think we made any difference?'

'We won some battles and lost others. Lesbians and gay men can celebrate their love and have children, and you see the odd black face on television, but zero-hour contracts have eroded rights the unions spent centuries fighting for. And more and more people are relying on food banks to feed their children.'

'Are you saying the battles we won were not of much consequence?'

'All we can hope to do is leave footprints that will lead future generations to venture further.' She puts down her glass of champagne, stands up and asks: 'Want to join me?'

'In what?'

'Dancing, of course. We'll dance to celebrate the life of a warrior.'

ABOUT THE AUTHOR

A writer from the west of Ireland, Miriam Burke's short stories have been widely published in anthologies and journals, including *The Manchester Review*, *Litro Magazine*, *Fairlight Shorts*, *The Honest Ulsterman*, *Bookanista* and *Writers' Forum*.

Miriam's short story 'A Splash of Words' was the runner-up for the 2011 Tom-Gallon Trust Award, and her work has been shortlisted for the *Mslexia* Short Story Competition, the William Trevor/Elizabeth Bowen International Short Story Competition, the *Grist Anthology of New Writing* competition and the novel category of the Yeovil Literary Prize.

Miriam has a PhD in Psychology, and before becoming a writer she worked for many years as a Clinical Psychologist in London hospitals and GP practices. *Women and Love* is her debut collection.

WWW.MIRIAMBURKEAUTHOR.COM